2022 SCI-FI ANTHOLOGY

SHORT STORIES BY SELECTED AUTHORS

E. J. RUNYON

S. A. GIBSON

PUBLISHED BY SCIENCE FICTION NOVELISTS 2022

CONTENTS

INTRODUCTION

In the Science Fiction Novelists Facebook group, we love saying "science fiction writers congregate, challenge, share, and compare," and with that in mind, we offer our finest for 2022. Our group is a place that fosters writing, imagination, and hope for mankind—though some of us may have destroyed the universe a few times.

Each year we challenge our members to submit their newest short stories. Gathered here are the imaginary worlds we create and have access to via our online world: thirteen stories from ten authors, spanning fantasy, speculative fiction and hard science fiction. Each story is original. This is our second volume, and hopefully not the last.

Significant credit goes to our two professional editors, E. J. Runyon and Katherine Kirk, also members of the group. They provided their services gratis, bringing polish and shine to this volume, and working with each author to bring all the stories to full flower without trampling on the writer's style.

We hope you enjoy spending time in these worlds.

A NOTE ON LANGUAGE

The Science Fiction Novelists group has members based all over the world who write in a variety of Englishes. This anthology features stories (and spelling) in British English and American English.

THE EDITORS

EDITOR IN CHIEF: S. A. GIBSON

S. A. Gibson has published more than ten books and several short stories, many co-written. Most stories are set in a future which has lost its advanced technology because of a catastrophic viral pandemic that has led to the collapse of modern civilization. Gibson uses his PhD in education to blend technological and historical research with creative ideas. Find out more about his work at www.protectedbooks.org.

DEVELOPMENTAL EDITOR: E. J. RUNYON

E. J.'s writing guides are *Tell Me (How to Write) a Story*, from Inspired Quill out of the UK, and *5 Ways of Thinking to Change Your Writing World Around* from Protected Books, in California.

She also has four well-regarded novels out from small indie presses. She's run the Bridge to Story website since 2010, where she coaches live, via Skype, and story edits both novices and published authors. Her life's goal is sharpening your stories into something deeper, to give your readers satisfying storytelling. Being notoriously *lysdexic*, E. J. never offers to proofread or line edit.

You can find her on social media, or at her website, which offers 52 free writing lessons: www.bridgetostory.com.

COPYEDITOR: KATHERINE KIRK

Kath works with publishers and independent authors on a wide range of genres, but she has a soft spot for the innovation at the core of science fiction and fantasy. She also edits tabletop role-playing content for game publishers and indie game magazines. She's lived all over the world and currently herds commas halfway up a volcano in Ecuador. She's an active member of the Chartered Institute for Editing and Proofreading, and you can find her talking about conscious language, games, and editing on Twitter (@KathLDK) or get in touch through her website: www.geckoedit.com.

SEARCHERS
MARC NEUFFER

Author of eight novels, Marc Neuffer uses his extensive science and engineering background to pen novels of future time and space with plausible science as a backdrop for his imaginative character-driven stories. Before becoming an author, Marc spent twenty years roaming the world with the US Navy as a nuclear propulsion engineer. He has lived in San Diego, Los Angeles, San Francisco, and Seattle. After retiring a second time, he bought a piano and started writing fun-read science fiction novels. With nothing else left on his bucket list, he dreams of future things to come. Find out more at www.m-c-neuffer.com.

Don't breathe. Don't twitch. Keep your slicer ready.

It was a rookie move, being so far into this twisted underground of deserted warrens and passages. Casey's guts twisted and fright flew electric as she pressed against the wire mesh barrier, regretting going down an unfamiliar maintenance tunnel. The smell of lubricant and the harsh scrapes of slithering tendrils across bare metal chilled her sweat-soaked skin. Twenty meters away, the hulking thing was sniffing along her carbon dioxide trail.

Need space. Need time.

Her breathing filter hung around her neck. The upper strap had failed, fatigued by too many days' exposure to acid air. Fingers inched to her vest pocket, knuckle creep by knuckle creep, for a decoy canister. In the dim light, two rats ran across the toes of her boots. Casey's natural response was to crush their little skulls; they ate her food, gnawed wires. But rats were harmless compared to what was seeking her. She didn't flinch, let them pass as they fled certain death.

A thundering reverberation and subterranean shaking showered her in dust and rust flakes. Hoping the roiling noise would cover her movements, she tossed the canister around the corner, discharging a carbon dioxide fog to divert the searcher.

Casey ran. One hand held the mask against her face. The other bumped along the dank wall to her right. This was an inbound access, slanting downward. If there were any traps, she knew those would be on the left. She'd been through other tunnels like this, decks littered with shredded mechanical bodies. The searchers never caught on.

Casey bumped into a ladder welded to the bulkhead. An open hatch, too small for the searcher to ooze through, was close above. The glimpse she'd had of her pursuer confirmed something was building more of these creepers. The new units were a better design, shiny, not cobbled together from old parts.

Once through, she slammed the scuttle shut, not caring about noise as she spun the dogging wheel tight. Wiping sweat from her eyes, she squatted and set to work repairing her mask. Every harvester had a healthy dread of acid lung, a debilitating, wasting walk to premature death. Before moving on, she reached for her canteen and discovered it missing from the rig slot.

2

Too far from a clean water source, she had to turn back early. Mitch would be pissed about the lost bottle, but the treasures in her bag should soften that anger—she'd avoid a beating. Casey stood, read the sensor pack screen, set her bearings, and started for home. She hoped there'd be enough water to rinse off the three-day grunge from harvesting in the dead zone. *Probably not*, she guessed. Not for one like her.

Except for the searchers, Casey liked not having to rely on anyone. When away from home, exploring and gathering, she considered the dead spaces her private domain.

* * *

"Whatcha got?" Mitch was never one to welcome a harvester home, never one to lose sleep over those who hadn't come back. Distracted by the bauble Casey held out, he didn't spot her missing canteen. She shifted, hiding the empty harness slot from his probing eyes.

"Some hand tools, a few manuals, and this control circuit board for a fabricator."

"Does it work?"

"How would I know? Everything's dead, except some lighting."

"Watch your mouth."

Casey knew she was edging toward insubordination and a face slap, but she was too drained to care. "The machinery's in decent shape but needs a jack crew to bring it home."

"Anything else?"

"Some canister caps and a roll of plastisheet. The thin kind."

"In three days, that's all you recovered?" He stared her down until she dropped her head. "All right, log those in and give 'em to Leroy."

"Water stocks?"

"Still low. No washing today. The tankmen are due back

3

tomorrow. They found a source deeper in, cleaner. Now, get going."

Out of Mitch's sight, she took a detour through a passageway choked with boxes, crates, and barrels, looking for a welcoming face. Rig Master Wanda had taken this urchin under her wing when Casey's mother failed to return twelve years ago. Sliding open the metal gate to Wanda's territory was like finding an oasis. Even the air tasted better here.

"How was it?" Wanda asked.

"More searchers. New ones, quicker."

"Crap. Did you tell Mitch?"

"Hell no! He'd want me to bring one back. I'll trickle it down to the clave."

"How was the air? Any better?"

"Worse. I used up six purifier packs. Was on my last one when I reached home."

Wanda slid a slate over to her. "You're due for a replacement rig. Take off your harness so I can do inventory."

Casey unbuckled and unstrapped, then slung her rig on the counter. "Got any new boots?"

"Not much call for your small size, but yeah, I put a pair aside for you. Best ones to come through here for some time." She examined Casey's rig, checking off each item. "Where's your bottle? You need to turn it in."

"Lost it in a chase."

Wanda reached into a bin and pulled out a crushed canteen. "I'll throw this in. The boys in repair will never know." She tapped the slate. "Sign the inventory."

Casey pressed her thumb on the scratched plastic. "Thanks. I've got too many work-off points as it is."

"Who, Mitch?"

"Don't say anything to him. Just make things worse."

"If it keeps up, I'll recycle one or two of his kidneys or toss a fragger under his bunk." Wanda grabbed a new rig from the shelf and dropped it on the counter. "Need gloves?"

4

"No. These are still okay, thanks," said Casey.

"Don't mention it, especially to Mitch. He's got something going on, and it won't be pleasant for anyone but him. You headed to Dev's?"

"Yeah. We're still cohabbing."

Wanda's nose scrunched. "You might want to wash the stink off first."

"Mitch said no washing until the tankmen come back."

"He's lying. Bet he's auctioning off your clave's supply. We have plenty. Use the shower here. I got some of that nice soap again."

"That'd be great. Hot?"

"Warm. Heater needs a new coil, but you won't freeze your ass off. See if you can find a replacement on your next run. Dev's place have water?"

"No, not rated for it."

"Towel rags are in the bin. If you have time, toss your clothes in the tumbler. They stink as bad as you do."

* * *

In the darkness, Casey rested her head in the nook of Dev's bare shoulder as they caught their breath.

"We think we're near to breaking through," he said. "Lots of damage and scrap in the way. Closed off deliberately."

"Bones?"

"Yeah, some. Gnawed."

Casey liked listening to Dev talk about his jack crew work, enjoyed the close rhythm as his chest rose and fell. When they were together, she could push aside worrisome thoughts and terrible memories. Casey reached between the wall and the thin pallet. "Saved this for you." She found Dev's hand and put a veggie bar in his palm.

Dev shifted. "This from your harvesting duty rations? Supposed to turn those in. You'll be in trouble again."

"They're to keep up our enzyme levels. I'm small, don't need so many. Nobody frisks us, and Wanda doesn't care. Anyway, I don't like the red ones. Too salty."

"Want me to wake you before my shift?"

"Yeah, I want to talk with Emma."

Casey fell asleep in the safest place she knew.

* * *

Daily clave gatherings weren't joyful occasions. They served as communal feedings, exchanges of gossip, and wonderings of what happened to those missing or still harvesting in the empty.

"Jad, you seen Emma?" Casey asked.

He raised his chin. "Over by the serving line, last I saw, talking to Bender."

"He's not part of our clave. What's a toolman doing here? Was he eating?"

"Relax, he's not taking any of our food. I think he's trolling for a new cohab."

Casey found Emma and Bender in huddled conversation. Didn't seem like a cohab negotiation to her, so she dropped her tray in next to them and sat on the bench. "What's doing?"

"Not much. You?" Emma's head swung around, checking who was nearby and might be listening.

"Got back yesterday from a three-day. New searchers again. Fast, not clunkers. Pass it along."

Bender's brow narrowed as he leaned in. "Where were you? What sector?"

"L. Up in the junker region."

"L section," Bender said. "I told you, Emma."

Casey moved closer. "Bender, what do you know?" For her and the other harvesters, new information about the upper spaces, any sliver of detail, might mean the difference between returning or being listed as lost.

"Tell her," Emma said. "Too many are wondering."

Bender's eyes took the same trip Emma's had, looking for eavesdroppers. "L, M, and N sections, the dead empty. Squad clave sent in six of theirs four days ago. Nobody's come back. The squads aren't talking, but my sister heard from a friend who cohabs with a squaddie. Something's going on."

Emma shuddered. "The machines."

* * *

"Dev, where's your group tunneling?" Casey asked.

"N3 quad, not far up. Why?"

"Emma and Bender think strange things are happening in the M, right next to where you guys are working."

"In the M? Naw. All crushed, according to the records. Bet the air's too polluted even for masks."

"My section is only one over, on the other side."

"Long way between L and M. Probably solid rock between them."

"So why is someone setting a perimeter with searchers? More aggressive ones."

"Someone? Come on, Casey. Those mechs are just holdovers, maintained by some automated repair unit up there. Can't be more than a few left now. Haven't found any in the N wedge."

"I've seen new searchers. Shiny, bigger." Casey propped up on her elbow. "Dev, one almost got me last time out."

"Why didn't you tell me before? Put in for a section transfer."

"Mitch won't approve it. Listen, I got a two-day before I go out again. Take me to where your crew's pushing through."

"Have to be third shift when no one's working."

"Fine with me. I'll bring my sensor gear."

"We got some units on-site," said Dev.

"But nothing portable. I want to do a deep snoop."

"Okay, but nothing dangerous."

"Sure. Just a look-see."

* * *

Dev swung his leg over a warped support beam and reached back for Casey's hand. Stark shadows moved in the shifting light of their headlamps. Metal creaked.

"This is as far as we can go. Too much blockage ahead," said Dev.

"I've been in tighter crawls than this. I'm gonna check it out, see how far back I can get."

Before he could object, all but Casey's feet disappeared under a tilted structural block. In a few seconds, she wiggled further in, out of sight.

"Come on, Dev," Casey's voice echoed back. "There's a void tall enough to stand in. Only four meters from you. Careful of the snags."

Dev crouched. Casey's light shone at a narrow bend. In a flat elbow and knee crawl, he maneuvered around it.

"Nothing here. Why'd you want me to come through?"

"Over here, behind this slab. A hatch. Doesn't seem damaged."

"Don't open it. You don't know what's on the other side."

Casey held up her sensor probe, waved it at him. "That's why we have this. Standard kit for harvesters."

"Won't tell you what's on the other side with the hatch shut."

"Yes it will, soon as I make a hole."

Dev shook his head. "You can't drill through. Too thick."

"Sure I can. I've done this before." Casey tapped her finger. "Right here, next to the dogging lever. Thin spots on each side of the door where the internal cam mechanism slides. Should punch through easy. I need you to dribble some lube while I drill."

Casey squatted and leaned in, centering her tool in the small divot she'd punched in the metal. She increased her drill speed, being careful not to snap the thin bit.

"Squirt some lube. This is just a pilot hole." A patient minute later, the drill hit air. Casey mounted a larger spiral cutter. "One more after this to make a hole large enough for the probe. Put your mask on." Casey reached into a vest pouch, handed Dev a small gray cylinder. "Hold this."

"What is it?"

"Plug goop. Have it ready when I break through."

Casey began drilling again. Once through, her eyes studied the sensor readout. Three greenies: negative explosive gases, negative acid, positive breathable.

"Everything's okay. Pressure's equal on both sides." She enlarged the holes to accommodate a fiber-optic scope. Pushing it through, she peered into the darkness. The next probe was a microphone. She listened—nothing. Sliding a switch sent a series of high-frequency sound waves into the void on the other side. As her sensor pack analyzed the return, she sat back, waiting.

"Crap!"

"What? What?" Dev demanded.

"Calm down. Check behind the wall plate."

Dev jerked his head around. "What?"

"The manual equalizing valve is sheared off. We didn't need to go through all this. I wondered why the pressure was equal and the atmosphere was the same on both sides. You ready? My readings show a short tunnel. Must be an airlock."

"All right, but be careful. Want me to lead?"

"No, I've got more experience in this sort of thing."

Casey heaved the dogging lever with a shoulder shove and swung the hatch inward.

She stepped over the threshold, scanning with her head-light, and spotted the equalizing valve at the next hatch. "Put your mask back on." With a quick open-shut, she ran more air samples. "Some airborne dust and rust, but nothing bothersome." Before Dev could object, Casey opened the hatch to a long corridor.

She stood ready to slam it shut if her sensor pack detected a searcher or movement of any kind. Their headlamps showed a dusty hallway, ending at a T intersection. Casey hesitated, then rolled a sensor ball along the passageway, aiming for a rebound into the right-hand passage to monitor both ways.

"Infrared clear, no motion. Let's go."

To the left of the T was another hatch. The right, like a dark maw, opened a huge, multilevel space. Casey set a thick bead of glue on the left hatch to keep anyone or anything from getting through without making a racket. She left the remote in the passageway, set to alert, before they moved to the metal cavern.

From the entry, the pair swept the interior with light. Casey tossed another sensor ball. The place was empty except for catwalks around the upper five floors. The open passages on each level made Casey's skin crawl. Any of those could hide searchers. She waited, listened, watched the readouts, felt Dev's breath on her neck. She was used to waiting. He wasn't. Ignoring Casey's hissed warning, he stepped over the hatch coaming and strode into the room, his footsteps echoing.

At the center, he turned to fill the upper levels with light. "All clear. Dead as a tomb." Casey wished he'd picked another word. She joined Dev as he shone his light straight up a hundred meters, illuminating a segmented dome ceiling.

Casey hugged herself. "Too big. I don't feel safe here."

"Looks like the roof retracts. What do you think?"

"I've never seen this sort of construction. Not a trace of acid air. Must be an open connection to our ventilation system." Casey backed up, close to the tunnel entrance they'd come through, her eyes sweeping the upper levels. "Or this section has a working one of its own."

Dev pointed to a series of stairs. "Want to go up?"

"No, too hard to climb down to an escape route. We'll take the passage opposite the way we came."

Dev walked to the other passage. "Some lighting systems are still powered farther on. Air's flowing in that direction too."

She followed, jogging across the cavern's floor.

* * *

Casey stopped, moved her hand behind, placing it against Dev's chest. They'd walked this path for two kilometers. "Wait. Smell that?"

Dev sniffed. "No."

She checked the remote they'd left behind. Still clear. "Something's not right. Take a knee against the bulkhead. Make yourself small." She kissed a third sensor ball before tossing it into the dark corridor. It was her last one. The rolling sound and her rushing heartbeat filled her ears.

Checking the sensor's video, Casey released her breath. "Now we know what happened to the squaddies. Place is blown to bits, and so are they. Must have been the rattle and shake I felt a few days ago." Casey used her pad to rotate and move the ball. On the viewscreen, six bodies lay sprawled on the deck. The walls were charred black, and a pipe had pulled free from its brackets, the ruptured ends ragged and bloomed out. "All shot to hell, too. They used kinetic rounds."

Casey traced the broken pipe back to where they stood, seeing a hydrogen icon stencil every five meters.

"Whatever it was, someone missed. Hit the gas line. Boom. I don't see any debris from what they thought was there. Might be further in. Can't get a remote connection to their gear. I'm going in."

"No, wait."

"You can stay, but I'm not leaving my last remote. We may need it. Besides, this happened days ago. Sensors say all clear."

The pair slow-stepped into the carnage and knelt by the first squaddie. He lay facedown, the back of his rig melted. Dev rolled him over, exposing a weapon, gear belt, and puffy, red-skinned face. "Ever seen this face?"

"No, but I don't hang with squaddies."

"I'm taking his weapon. We may need it."

"You know how to use it?"

"Had some training a few years ago, when I thought about joining up. His rig's got three ammo canisters. Should we bag a weapon for you?"

"No. Wanda slipped me a few fraggers when I told her where we were going. I wanted someone to know in case we didn't come back. I'm gonna try a line-link to this guy's rig."

Casey heard Dev gag as he rolled over the other squaddies. Except for the first one, furthest from the blast, the squaddies' gear and bodies were burned, blackened. White-faced, Dev came back to Casey. "No signs of them being in a close fight. You got anything on the vid?"

Casey ran a jack line to the fallen squaddie's rig, and Dev studied the video screen over her shoulder.

"Fast forward. Find when they entered this passage," said Dev.

They watched the video of the last man in line. Everything seemed normal until a squaddie yelled, "Contact, front!" and began firing. His teammates jumped to hug the walls on either side, firing at something. Then a huge shake and fireball erupted. Silver metal flashed across the screen and was gone.

"What were they shooting at?"

"A searcher, I'll bet. The others started firing, hit the gas line. Everything before was normal-normal. Must have made a hell of a hot flash-out."

"Let's move on."

Dev hesitated. "They *were* shooting at something."

"That was days ago. Come on." Twenty meters along the passage, they found scattered metal parts.

12

"Look at the size of that pincher," said Dev.

Casey kicked the claw to the side. "One of the new ones. It got away."

They moved on, moved up, far into the dead zone.

* * *

"Good a place as any to sleep." Casey wiggled through a ventilation slot to a plenum inlet large enough to stretch out in.

"Jacker boss is gonna be mad I'm not working," said Dev.

"I got you covered. Had Wanda put you on the medical list for three days."

"Three? You planned for us to be gone three days?"

"Said I got you covered. We need some rest." Casey wagged her eyebrows. "Or do you want to fool around first?"

"I'm not taking my clothes off for anything until we're back home."

Casey grinned. "Don't say I didn't offer."

"Do you even have a plan? I mean, an actual plan? We've been moving upward all day."

Casey checked the feed from the remote she'd left on the deck outside. "That's the plan. As long as we can find water, up we go. Settle in. I'll take the first watch."

Casey chewed a carb bar, keeping her eyes glued to the sensor pack screen. She didn't wake Dev when a trio of small searchers marched past their night hole. The last one clutched a dead rat on its back.

* * *

Dev rubbed his sore legs as Casey wiped grime from the hatch window. Bringing her face to the glass, she said, "People! There are people in there."

She stood aside to let Dev peek through the round viewport. The well lit scene was strange to Casey. Their gear, equipment, and clothing looked unfamiliar. New. Not cobbled together from salvage. Not patched and repatched.

Dev moved his face from the small window. "I don't recognize their clothing. Everyone's wearing the same thing, geared out the same. I count ten. You?"

"Yeah, six men, four women, no children. They're eating. I didn't see any weapons, but they have crates marked explosive." Casey grabbed the hatch wheel.

Dev placed his hand over hers. "I don't think we should go in. They could be dangerous."

"I don't think so. They don't move around like squaddies, and four of them are old. Stay here, keep your weapon ready." Casey swung the hatch open.

* * *

Hinges squealed. Hector turned. He was surprised to find two ragged, dirt-smudged people standing by an open hatch. One of them held a gun. He lifted his hands to shoulder level while others sought cover behind equipment boxes. Four ran for the opposite passageway.

"Hello. Care to join us?" It was the only thing Hector could think to say, knowing this place was supposed to be deserted. No squatters or resettlers were within two thousand miles of this squashed place. Hector eyed the nervous young man near the hatch, watching the shifting weapon, pointed down but ready.

The young woman took a few tentative steps forward. "Who are you? What clave? What are you doing here?"

"My name's Hector. We're exploring these ruins for the historical society. How did you get in here? How long have you been hiding in this wreckage?"

The pair looked at each other, then back at Hector. "I'm Casey, and this is Dev. This is our home."

"Please, come sit. Would you like to eat? We have food prepared." Hector spread his hands. "Join us?"

Casey sniffed the air, stepped closer. Dev edged a step back to the hatch.

Hector turned his back, called to his companions. "Come out, everyone. You're hiding like frightened children." Hector hoped his words would fortify his group and soothe the visitors. Casey continued toward Hector. A friendly sign. "How long have you been here?" he asked.

Casey tilted her head. "All my life. Nine generations, I guess. Since the collapse."

"Collapse? You must mean the asteroid strike."

"Yeah. Were there other survivors? Outside? The planet didn't die?"

Hector's eyes widened. "Originals," he called out, "Kate, these are originals! Next time you go topside, call this in." He turned back to Casey. "Several billion survived. Lots of quake damage, but most people moved before the impact, spread out away from the coasts. Some sheltered in prepared undergrounds like this one. How many of you are in this mash-up?"

"Almost fifteen hundred." Casey hung her head. "There used to be more."

"We can take everyone to a better place," Hector offered.

Scritchy mechanical sounds came from an upper level as a huge searcher slithered from a dark passage. Casey ran toward the hatch as Dev fired, shredding the monster.

"Hey, hey!" shouted Hector. "Stop shooting, stop shooting!"

"A searcher!" Casey screamed. "Those things are deadly. Haven't you seen them before?"

"You mean the quads? We use them to clear heavy debris and jack up passages. We use smaller ones to keep the vermin away during explorations. Lots of rats in here."

"Those things have been killing us! Did you bring them? Why?"

"Killing? Not possible," Hector said, countering Casey's explosive statement.

Casey hesitated for a moment. "They've been killing us since the collapse, every chance they get. They kill on sight."

"Not ours. We brought them in only three weeks ago."

Turning to Dev, Casey said, "That was one of the new ones I've seen on my last runs."

Hector's eyebrows raised. "Have any of these harmed anyone?"

"We always run. No one's been killed in a few years."

"Yando, bring me a delta unit." The woman Hector motioned to opened a case, removed a small blocky thing, and handed it to Hector. The cube unfolded in his hand. Stumpy legs emerged, followed by tentacles, waving, sensing. "See? Harmless, except to rats and such. Here, take it."

Casey backed away from the miniature horror.

Hector put the crawler back in its box. "Have you ever been outside?"

Casey shook her head. "No one goes outside. Everyone knows it's a wasteland. Broken bare rock, glassy surfaces, radiation. Nothing alive. Safer here."

"There's no radiation hazard. Never was. But you're right about this sector. Life is coming back at the edges, a long way from here." Sensing their unease, seeing their wary eyes, he asked, "Would you like to see?"

* * *

Hector took the young pair up a new lift to the surface. Casey gasped. Her knees weakened when she saw the blue sky. Overcome by the expanse, she grabbed for Dev to steady herself.

"Don't look up," Dev said, his voice shaky.

For a minute, they stood together in silence near the edge

of a recently carved ledge, ten steps from the deep shaft they'd ascended.

Breathless, Casey held tight to Dev's arm and whispered in his ear, "This place isn't for us. Too big. I don't feel safe."

"You gonna be okay?" he asked.

Her eyes went skyward. "Where does it end?"

Dev took a step closer to the rim, assessing the steep drop. He turned back to Casey. Her eyes passed information before they sought the ground again. He nodded.

Dev asked, "What's that? This thing under the ledge?"

Hector moved closer to see what Dev was pointing at. As he leaned over, a push from behind unbalanced him. Casey's second shove sent him tumbling to the craggy rocks below.

"Back down?" asked Dev.

"Yeah." Casey held Dev's hand as they stepped onto the lift.

"Might need to shoot a few." He jacked in a new magazine. "The rest can carry equipment back for us. We can stash it in the dome room and make them show us how to control their searchers. After that . . ."

Casey nodded. "After that, we bury them in rubble. With those explosives, we can bring down five levels. They'll never dig us out again."

Casey had bigger after-that plans beyond the immediate day. She smiled at the thought of tentacles wrapped around Mitch's neck.

As they descended, Dev kissed Casey's hand. "Let's go home."

LAST MISSION
S. A. GIBSON AND J. I. ROGERS

S. A. Gibson lives in California and has studied communication and computer science. His books and stories are set in a future world where advanced technology has been lost. Find out more about his work at www.protectedbooks.org.

J. I. Rogers is an award-winning author and artist who creates sci-fi, dystopian, cyberpunk, and mythologically themed works. Visit www.jirogers-author.com for links to social media and more.

Alfonso

The room the kidnappers shoved them into was through the small door of what seemed to be a storage shed. Streams of light leaked through a small, high window. Once the door had locked behind them, they just sat there.

"Are we out of time?" Alfonso wondered. He pushed the curls off his shoulders, not having anything else to ask.

"This looks ominous." Destiny paced as she answered,

waving around the dismal room. Bare walls, mostly clean, with two chairs and a table.

"You caught that slip, didn't you? They said *librarians*," Alfonso reminded his sibling. He thought of her as his sister. But looking at her, all he saw was the body he should have gotten two years ago, in the transfer gone wrong. He being in her host's body and vice versa.

"But the locals in town told us the Library has been kicked out of this area." Destiny combed strong fingers through her too-short hair. "Someone needs to tell these boys that. How's your head feeling?"

"Better, actually." He gave the truthful answer. "Letting Wynona have control for more time seems to help." It had been a battle, but Alfonso's male mind and psyche had come to terms with the female host he'd mistakenly landed in, although he still thought of himself as male, even with the curls.

It had been two years since that awful mix-up. His sister, residing in Jacob's body, continued to pace. She nodded and rubbed at her stubbled chin. Two very long years. "I've been finding the same thing." She lowered her voice. "Sharing my mind with Jacob allows me to hold onto more stability."

Alfonso sighed, in a higher register, and kept his hands in his lap, refusing to toss his long curls again. A sound alerted them to company.

Was it the kidnappers come back? No, though a couple did join them in the mostly empty room. These were newer faces. Both wore robes flowing down to their feet. *Actual Librarians!*

"Thanks for answering our summons." The woman announced, "I am Librarian Polar. This is Mister Bartholomew. We are glad to meet you."

The siblings exchanged glances but kept silent, simply waiting. What was the ploy these people were playing at? Finally, Destiny answered, "What do you want? Your thugs weren't very talkative." Her fist clenched.

The man spoke up. "Ah, I see." He offered another bow. "We apologize. As you may have heard, we have been stripped of authority in the Pacific Northwest."

Polar added, "And therefore must operate in the shadows." At their unchanged frowns, she continued, "We have less choice of who we hire to be our eyes, ears, and hands."

Alfonso was thinking they might survive. *Surely the librarian would not waste time sharing information if she was going to order us killed.*

"What do you want of us?" Alfonso asked. He touched the growing bump on the back of his head. "Your minions gave us no clue."

The librarian's face seemed sad. She made a *may I sit?* gesture and lowered herself into a chair. "Unfortunately, we have a difficult task for you. Show them, Bartholomew."

The man drew a paper from his robe's sleeve, unrolling a drawing of a man. Young-looking. Bartholomew explained, "He calls himself Amaranth. This may or may not be hard for you to comprehend." This time, it was Polar and Bartholomew who exchanged a glance before he continued. "But he has access to technology no one in our time can understand."

"What do you mean?" Destiny added a sarcastic laugh. "You librarians are supposed to know all of the old tech."

Polar shook her head. "We don't know this. No one does. At least, until we heard tales of you two. We need your help. Hence the summons."

Summons? Try abduction. "Why do you think we can help?" Alfonso felt as puzzled as he sounded.

"Well, Des and Al, we have been investigating you two since you arrived mysteriously in the Pacific Northwest two years ago. We know about the bunker at the Hanford nuclear reactor facility that you broke into." Alfonso worked to avoid looking at Destiny. "Did you not realize it had been sealed with pre-Collapse tech? Activating those processes in that facility did what, neutralize dangerous chemicals? Having you on our side is important. You are the pair that likely saved thousands of lives."

Destiny looked to the little window and paused before responding. "What makes you think we were involved?"

Bartholomew now drew a stack of papers from another sleeve and all but waved it at the pair. "We've conducted extensive interviews with Vashon troopers, as well as other witnesses who place you there."

Alfonso's mind raced. *C'mon, brain. Time to think a way out of this.* He was answered by profound silence. *Damn. Time to stall.* "What do you want with these look-like-us people?"

Librarian Polar plucked one of the pages and smoothed it on the table. *Enough of this playacting.* "Here is a description of a device Amaranth is in possession of." She glanced to her partner. "And the pair of you may well know the danger we face. We believe he is able to use it to take over the minds of captives. After he uses it, his captive becomes a willing servant or ally. We wish you no harm, but we want you to destroy this device, no matter the reason for things you've done while here."

Alfonso struggled even more fiercely not to look at Destiny. Again, his sibling thought faster. "That sounds impossible. Crazy. How can anything mechanical do that to a mind?"

Librarian Polar's intense stare focused on Destiny first, and then Alfonso. He tried to not react, to keep his breathing even. "Nevertheless, that is the description we have heard. We sent in a trusted agent to investigate. Now Sharona seems to have become a willing servant of Amaranth."

"Have you told the local authorities?" Destiny asked. "They have police, militia, and full military units."

Polar shook her head again. "We've learned the Vashon military command have experienced the same setback we have. They've sent in operatives who have been converted. To a man, their loyalties have been destroyed."

Sounds dangerous in more ways than one. Being found out

would be the least of our worries, if this is true. We've got to get out of doing this. "And you expect us to stop this . . . madman? Us? By ourselves?" He was trying to get out of doing this job. All to no avail.

Librarian Polar was having none of it. A raised hand to the pair, and a *bunk-bunk-bunk* of fingers on the stack of papers, brought Alfonso's protests to a halt.

"We're assembling a strike team to go in with you," Bartholomew reassured the pair. "It's been difficult, since we have to operate in secret, but by tomorrow, we should have a dozen fighters who can help you."

Finally, Alfonso let himself share a glance with Destiny. He raised an eyebrow and noted the slight nod. "Can we have a minute to talk this over? Alone?"

"Of course." The librarian rose and led Bartholomew out, pausing only to add, "Your service will save the Pacific Northwest. Maybe the world."

* * *

Destiny

It was a relief to escape that room.

"Librarians *are* scary." Destiny glanced back at their two bodyguards. Starling and Nora were to help them make contact with the strike team. She suspected they were also there to prevent her and Alfonso from bolting from the assignment. At least they stayed a meter back as they walked where Starling had pointed. It might have been another librarian safe house, for all she knew.

"How much do you think the librarian knows? About us, our botched transfers?" Alfonso kept his voice low.

Destiny frowned. "Nothing, I hope. I don't think so, anyway. But I couldn't stop thinking about it the whole time we were in there."

"Exactly," Alfonso agreed. "I wonder if Amaranth had the same issue we did when he was sent back. Do you think they suspect him of also being sent?"

Destiny snuck a nervous glance back. "It certainly sounded like it. But I don't recognize his name, and from the image, his face, either. Of course, we wouldn't."

"When we were implanted in these bodies, the machine shut down," Alfonso reminded her. "How could *he* use it over and over again? Wouldn't his machine lose power too?"

Destiny scratched her stubble. "No. The machine left us to find a hiding place to shut down. Technically, it was still operational. We expected it to power down. But we didn't witness it."

"I never even considered the idea of re-implanting our consciousnesses in other bodies." Alfonso sounded upset. His step quickened. "I'm still apologizing to Wynona for stealing her body and her life."

"I know. I have the same conversation in my head with Jacob," Destiny answered. "A stolen life. And I can never give his body back to him. Not without dying myself."

This time, when Destiny looked back, Nora pointed to the right, so they headed down that side street. The town of Bend, Oregon, was much smaller than before the Collapse, but thousands of people did live here. Only a few were out this late in the evening. They'd seen one patrol of Vashon police.

Starling joined them and beckoned them over to a darkened doorway. Alfonso and Destiny stood back as Nora and Starling took positions on either side. Nora rapped a complicated series of knocks on the door, and they waited. A series of return knocks came from inside. The two seemed to relax as the door was opened. It dawned on Destiny then that neither Starling nor Nora wore anything visible to identify themselves as librarians.

This room was full. Nora waved her hand around at the

people squeezed in. Each carried weapons: swords, bows and arrows, and staffs.

"We have two squads. I lead one group; Starling leads the other. Everyone, this is Des and Al. They will be coming along." Nora introduced her team, followed by Starling introducing his. Most were young men and women, with a few older members.

"This is Christina." Starling pointed to a woman dressed in Vashon uniform. "She's undercover. She'll send in a Vashon army group after the fight starts." Destiny looked at her brother and thought, *if they have undercover Vashon, they intend on taking this fellow out.*

Seemed like that would be bad for the librarians. *Guess they're willing to risk it. They really care about saving lives.*

"What's the plan?" Destiny asked.

"That's why you're here," Christina answered. "You tell us."

Nora unrolled a large sheet on the table. "This is a drawing of the compound at Sisters. Our main concern is that Amaranth will be able to get the machine away, out of Oregon."

Destiny pulled Alfonso over to study the schematic. Starling nudged Nora out of the light. Alfonso poked a finger at a room on the drawing, looking to his sister for silent confirmation.

Destiny nodded, moving her hand over the right side of the map, tapping twice. She looked to Starling. "One of us needs to go in before the attack."

"Why?"

"We need someone to find the machine before Amaranth knows there's a threat," she explained, "then prevent the device being removed as the attack commences. Do you have someone who can back me up? I'll do it."

Alfonso shook his head vigorously. "No. I'm the better

fighter." Destiny took a long time deciding. She knew what Alfonso was not saying. She understood the tech of the device better and would be more help in the long term, if the machine slipped through their hands.

Finally, she nodded. "Very well, sister. Your sacrifice will be remembered . . ."

Nora and Starling exchanged a puzzled glance. Then Nora asked, "What's the best way to destroy this . . . machine?"

Destiny started. "I imagine it is a sphere, maybe about half a meter wide." She held her hands apart and raised her eyebrows with a shrug. "If so, we need to puncture it. We should drive something straight into the center of the device. If the wiring and circuitry can be damaged enough, no one in this time will ever be able to get it working again."

"How can you know that?" Starling cocked his head with his question.

"That's why we're here." Alfonso straightened his shoulders. "According to the reports, we're the experts."

"Everyone, get some rest," Nora ordered. "We'll start at dawn. Should get to Sisters by the afternoon."

* * *

Alfonso

"Looks like the surface of the moon." Alfonso's gaze swept the landscape. They'd been walking for seven hours.

"Lava Lands," Starling informed him. His arm stretched toward the hills and vast fields of broken black rocks. "Before the Collapse, astronauts used to train here to prepare for going to the moon or Mars."

"Well, somehow it's fitting, considering our mission." Alfonso seemed to be speaking only to himself.

"I'm worried about you," Destiny told him, again.

"We're close now, right?" Alfonso asked. *C'mon. Keep it together. I just have to stay alive and keep them from mind-wiping me before you come in with the cavalry. What could possibly go wrong?* Alfonso couldn't stop a laugh.

Nora waved to a stand of trees struggling in this wasteland. Several in the group shielded their eyes from the setting sun. "We'll set up camp here, wait until night for the armed team to go in. We don't want to spook our target."

"Al and I need to make some final plans," Destiny told Nora. "We'll be over there." She pointed out a clearing among the black rocks. At Nora's nod, they set off.

"I can't help feeling awful about Wynona and Jacob. They didn't sign up for any of this," Alfonso confided.

"Yes. That's what I wanted to say." Destiny's frown reinforced her worry. "We need to consult with them about this mission."

"Their choices are fewer than ours in this."

"Still, they need to be in on the decision," Destiny insisted. "If we die, they die with us."

Alfonso chose a large rock to sit on. Jagged and painful. And hot. "How do you want to do this?"

"Let's try trading off," she decided. "I'll speak to Wynona. Then you can talk to Jacob."

"This'll take me a minute." Alfonso breathed deeply and focused on drifting away into a trance. It had taken them months to figure out how to give the original occupants of these bodies the ability to control their former flesh. It still wasn't easy. Still a work in progress.

"Ah!" Wynona shook her head like a wet dog.

"Wynona?"

"I miss having a body." Alfonso could hear the words and see Destiny through Wynona's eyes, but he was just an observer. Now he couldn't speak or move her limbs. It was a fearful feeling, every time.

"I'm so sorry," Destiny said. Her face showed her deep sorrow. "We stole your body."

"Not you. Alfonso." Wynona's voice rang with accusation.

"You know what I mean." Destiny repeated a conversation they'd shared before. "Alfonso and I deprived you and your brother of your lives."

Again, Wynona spoke out from within Alfonso's body. "I know." She shook her head and made him grimace. "I'm not mad anymore. *Much.*" Absently, she looked over to the armed group setting up tents. "It's just so terrible being trapped and not in here, when I'm not running things in my own body."

"I know. I can't imagine how you survived. Alfonso and I were trained. We knew we'd lose our bodies and take over new ones after years of being frozen in stasis." Destiny watched that the others, a few meters away, were not paying attention to this conversation. "But you two had no idea what was happening." She hated to, but she confided, "We didn't even know you'd survive. For days afterward, we were sure you were completely gone."

"And now you're about to risk losing our bodies again." Wynona jabbed an accusing finger Destiny's way.

Destiny gave a sad, apologetic shiver. "Well, I'm asking now. Do you agree with us? Going on this mission?" Again, a glance toward the armed team only steps away. "To stop this man who calls himself Amaranth? If you say no, Alfonso and I will try to back out, give them only the info they need. It's your body. You need to give permission. We'll run away, if possible."

Wynona hung her head, deep in thought. Destiny thought about how the Collapse had changed everything. When she and Alfonso were packed into the machine, it was just beginning. The virus was spreading around the world. Civilization was falling apart. The technological knowledge that had allowed scientists to embed minds into a machine was far beyond any that now remained.

"Well, as you and Alfonso said, we have no choice," Wynona finally spat out.

"It seems that way . . ." Destiny counted the librarian team members in case Wynona said no. "Say the word. We can try to get away. Most people say the Library isn't cruel with punishments, so I don't expect they'd kill us. They'd probably just make us pay in other ways."

"No," Wynona conceded. "You and Alfonso are probably the best people in the world to fix this problem. The mission seems important."

Destiny let out the breath she didn't realize she was holding. "I wanted to ask you about that. Do you remember anything of Alfonso taking over your mind and body?"

"No." Wynona shook her head with a sad smile. "I was sleeping. When I woke, I was deep out of control, only vaguely able to see what was happening. Like I wasn't in my own body."

"You were probably lucky." Destiny bit down on her lip, guilt rising all over again. "It must have been a painful process."

"Don't you know? Didn't the scientists tell you what happened to . . . test subjects?" That stopped Destiny for a moment. *She probably got that term from Alfonso's mind.*

"They didn't tell us anything about what the hijacked mind would feel. Probably didn't want us thinking too much about how we were overwriting people." Destiny wrestled her mind away from that. "But Alfonso might need your help. If you are put under the machine, you've got to work together with him to resist Amaranth taking over. Do you have any ideas that might help?"

Wynona pursed her lips and rubbed her chin. "When I'm in control, I can pretty much resist Alfonso coming back by focusing on my muscles, my entire body."

Destiny did her best to avoid thinking about what

Wynona's words meant. *She'd resisted?* "So whichever of you is in control needs to hold that against Amaranth's invading mind." She thought a minute. "If one of you gets kicked out, the other needs to take over. You must not let go. Will you do that, Wynona?"

"Yes." Her grave expression promised more than that single word.

"Thank you. We will owe you forever. Can you please let Alfonso come back?" Destiny tried a warm smile. "I'll switch over to Jacob, so they can talk—"

Wynona cut in, saying, "We haven't spoken in so long. Can Jacob and I have a moment? I miss him so much." Her words tugged at Destiny's heart.

"Of course. Just switch over when you're done."

* * *

Alfonso

Before dusk, having regained the body, Alfonso felt especially alone. The time he'd spent out of control made him wonder how Wynona could have stood it all these years. But there was no time to dwell on such things. The town of Sisters was bustling, many people hurrying on their own missions. Sisters, home to almost one thousand people now, so long after the Collapse, was thriving. Alfonso stopped a well-dressed woman striding by.

"Excuse me, miss. I understand Amaranth has meetings in town. I am looking to find him."

The woman gave his dress a jaundiced glance. "You're in luck. The charlatan is holding one of his public addresses right now. Just saw him at the band shell. Center of town." She pointed down the main street. "I hope the authorities put a stop to his lies and his lording it over everyone."

"Thank you, ma'am. Thank you."

The woman was right. Alfonso found a small crowd before the band shell. A man stood with arms raised, pontificating up there. He sounded fired up. He must have been winding up to a crescendo for a while.

"I am Jonas Hellman! I died and live again." That name sounded familiar, but Alfonso had never met Jonas in the past. "I was born before the Collapse. My mind was stripped out and put into a machine." He paused for dramatic effect. "That machine held my mind for almost one hundred years. Now, I am alive again. Now, my name is Amaranth!"

Mild applause rose, scattered through the group. Alfonso worked on picking out the people who'd already been taken over. The obvious ones were dressed as guards. Two stood to each side of the band shell. Others were sprinkled around the edges of the crowd. Alfonso estimated about half the people in this square already contained Amaranth's mind. Alfonso wondered how they got along. Did they share authority? Was talking to each other like talking to themselves? Or was the first one to be switched a dictator over the others? Alfonso felt Wynona's presence fluttering on the periphery of his consciousness. *She's listening too.*

A woman beside Alfonso raised her hand. "Excuse me. Why did they put your mind in a machine?"

Amaranth flashed some irritation before his serene expression returned. "I was sent on a mission to destroy a stockpile of nerve gas stored at the army depot at Umatilla."

Alfonso remembered hearing discussion of the potential mission. *Thought it had been shelved.* Not necessary, he had heard. He, too, raised his hand and risked asking, "Did you complete your mission?"

Amaranth cast an intense glare his way. Guards to the left and right of him followed that gaze. "No. Everyone who sent me here is dead. I am making my own destiny now."

Amaranth inspected the people in the crowd. *Probably looking for new converts.*

"You have a choice to make in your lives," Amaranth resumed. "You can continue living the same dull, boring way you are now, or you can join me. You can have a new life. You can become a new person!"

Alfonso inwardly nodded. *That's the truth.*

"What do we do?" another woman called out. Alfonso pegged her as one of Amaranth's converts. A plant.

"Stand over here, with Olivia. I will gather you up to me, and we can talk about how you can begin a new life."

Alfonso watched as a few people approached Olivia. He identified a few more as plants. He joined in. *Are they all him?* Wynona asked. *I don't know,* Alfonso replied. It was the truth; he didn't.

Inside a nearby building, like sheep, the small group was rounded up. Alfonso could hear the door lock behind them. *Only three recruits.* He thought the other two were surely plants, already converted.

Two guards threw open a door, and Amaranth strutted into the room, making eye contact with the new people before moving to stand on a small box. "You are beginning a new life. Only you will have access to the secrets we are revealing today! You will see wondrous things. Your friends and family will envy you." His arms swept up, like he was going to fly away. "You will be set free today!" Again, he met everyone's eyes, one by one. "Meet Olivia, my fellow leader. She will guide you through the first steps of the process. I will return to you after you have completed the most important step of your change."

Olivia was a well-dressed young woman. She raised her arms. In a moment, she'd introduced herself and explained how they would become part of a growing, powerful movement. Her mannerisms and speaking echoed the leader's.

This one is surely a copy of Amaranth.

"Has anyone received training in martial arts or weapons?" she asked. Alfonso noticed her intense examination of the three of them, but not the two plants. The sound of drums echoed in another room. And something else—maybe machinery?

Alfonso shook his head. *I've got to delay their wanting me as long as possible.* He thought of how the process worked. The implanted mind didn't normally have access to many of the memories of the host body. But the physical abilities of the host were more readily available. *So muscle memory is what Amaranth is looking for.*

One woman looked around before she raised her hand. Olivia led her over to another leader who took her out of the room.

"That is so wonderful," Olivia said. "Young Sarafina will be our first new member today. She will transform into a new person."

"What's that?" Alfonso pointed his chin to a thick cable snaking across the floor, along a wall, and between two doors.

Olivia's eyes bored into him for an instant. "That conducts what is called *electricity.*"

"What I thought." Alfonso nodded but kept his eyes away from the two doors. "I apprenticed for a time with an artisan. He used a steam engine to produce electricity."

Another intense stare. "Good to know. We can use skills like that."

Alfonso pretended to be excited by her pronouncement, but it puzzled him. *So, it's not just muscle memory they want. Technical skills are important too. But surely you can't acquire those if you implant over them?*

"Now, let me tell you about this new world we are building . . ." She droned on with poorly defined goals and plans. Alfonso wasn't sure what the point of her lecture was until a man came out of the back room that Sarafina had disappeared into. Getting Olivia's attention, he gave a nod. The lecture ended abruptly. *Ah, Sarafina is a new person!*

"James." She looked directly at the recruit standing next to Alfonso. "I'm interested in your story. Please tell me more about yourself." She cast a toothy smile on him.

* * *

Destiny

"I can't stand this waiting!" Destiny complained.

Nora nodded and adjusted the scabbard at her hip. "This is the hard part of any action." First pointing toward Three Sisters, one peak standing away from the other two along the ancient caldera, then to her armed team members lounging around, she explained, "It never gets easier."

"But he—my sister could be in danger. Can't we go in now?"

Nora pointed down toward the town in the distance. "We need to be able to approach the town without being observed. They'll have city guards at the gate."

Destiny's teeth hurt from her gritted jaw. She waved none too gently to the armed group. "Why not just fight our way in?"

Nora faced this anger with an open expression. "We don't want Amaranth to know we're coming. I understand the frustration, but now is the time for patience."

"Argh!" Destiny forced herself to take a deep breath and willed her hands to unclench. "How long?" *This is intolerable.*

Nora glanced up to the distant mountains. The sun was just touching them. "Almost dusk. Won't be long now."

And it wasn't. The long wait melted away. Soon the sun was lost behind the mountains. Breaking camp, the librarian's fighters traveled light. Most equipment was left cached among

33

the rocks. They stalked to a part of the town that was off the main road.

"How will we find Des?" Destiny had not calmed down. Her worry burned like a flame. "I can't lose my sister." She restrained herself from raising her voice. She was sensitive to their need to sneak into town and not set off alarms.

"We'll grab someone and ask." Nora shared a fierce grin with Destiny, her words trying to soothe. "It's our whole mission. When we find her, we find the device."

Instead of making Destiny feel better, that made her more nervous. Finding Alfonso meant finding the machine. *The machine that could even now be wiping his mind and Wynona's from their body.* "Let's hurry."

A low wall surrounded the town. Finding a makeshift passageway some enterprising townsperson had fashioned, their group passed quickly inside without alerting the town guards.

Crouching on a side street, in the growing darkness, Nora grasped Destiny's shoulder. "Will you be able to recognize the device if we find it?"

"Yes." Destiny abandoned caution. Her worry for Alfonso removed her concern for revealing their secret. "I'll know."

Nora's piercing gaze was visible in the shadows where they crouched. "Good." She signaled to one of the team, who approached. Nora relieved him of a long metal pole. "Will this work to destroy it?"

Destiny hefted the weapon she'd handed over, taking a few practice swings. "Yes. This should do nicely." She tried to remember the tensile strength or yield stress of the mind storage unit, but couldn't bring up any exact numbers, just that it was designed to be strong. "I'll have to hit it just right. Solid, focused blows." That was as precise as she felt she could be.

With a nod, Nora motioned Starling to move forward.

Someone was walking at the end of the street ten meters away. A small woman or child, Destiny thought.

In three quick steps, Starling dragged them back. It was a young woman. She looked terrified. Nora flashed a knife in front of her face. "We won't hurt you." *Mixed message*, Destiny thought. "We just need to know where Amaranth is. Which way to his house?"

The captive's eyes remained fearful, but her arm came up immediately, pointing down the street. At a sign from Nora, the man holding her removed his hand from the woman's mouth. "How do we get there?" he whispered.

"Ah . . . Just-just down two blocks. Wait. If you don't want to be seen . . ." She pointed behind her. "Behind this red house two blocks, then one block left."

Nora nodded her head, putting the knife away and twisting her face into a bit of a smile. Destiny thought it was still scary, that smile. "How will we know it?"

"It's green." The woman seemed to be relaxing somewhat. Her words came more evenly. "The ugliest green. Two stories. Only one on that block."

"Thank you." Nora nodded. "Go."

Moments later, they spied the house. It *was* ugly. In Destiny's mind, the machine inside made it uglier. Taking people's lives against their will. She suppressed the memories of her part in doing just that to Jacob. *Two years of making peace with this truth.*

Observing two guards outside the front door, Nora gave a complex series of hand signals to several of her fighters. Starling was the first to move quickly to the ugly green building.

* * *

Alfonso

Alfonso's nerves were at the breaking point. They'd taken James away. *That must have been half an hour ago.* There couldn't be much time remaining before Alfonso's turn.

Finally, Olivia paused in her long soliloquy about time, space, and the future. "Des." She ignored the others in the room. Flattering, in a way. All this theater just for one recruit. *Amaranth has a well-honed system.* "You know something about steam engines? And electricity?"

"Yes." Alfonso had to force himself not to sound too enthusiastic. *This was a good sign. Surely they couldn't use his knowledge if his mind was wiped.*

"Follow me." She turned without a pause, walking to a different door.

Alfonso restrained himself from running. He was supposed to find the machine. *But if I find it . . .* He shuddered at the implications.

Alfonso asked, "You have a steam engine here?" as they exited the room. Olivia didn't spare even a glance his way.

"You'll see. I want to see how much you know."

Before they reached it, he could hear the noise of an engine, smell the oil and burning wood. He remembered it well after these two years. "You know, after the Collapse, when petroleum products were forbidden," he babbled, "that was because of a civilization-destroying virus transmitted through gasoline and other similar products." He couldn't stop himself and ended lamely, "So these days, steam engines burn wood or charcoal."

Heat blasted Alfonso's face. A lone woman sat in a chair in the corner of the room, which was large, mostly taken up with a squat boiler filling more than half the space. The woman's face was smudged and streaked with black, like everything else in the room.

"What is that?" Olivia pointed to the large tank.

"The main boiler." *So this is a test.* Alfonso needed to pass. *But if I pass, will it keep me away from the machine?*

"And that?" She pointed up to an open pipe near the top. Alfonso couldn't decide if he should pass or fail.

"Looks like an emergency venting outlet."

"What about that?" She pointed over to one corner of the space.

"Ah." Alfonso stepped over. "Amazing." It was small, only about the size of a cedar hope chest. Though no one would imagine *this* sitting at the end of a bed, filled with linens. A rod passed from the steam engine into one side of it. Wires snaked out the back. "A generator. I've never seen one so small."

Her eyes bored into him. "You know a great deal about this." She waved over the woman in the corner. "Edith." At that word of command, the woman looked up, fear in her eyes. She knew exactly what to do. She stood up, moving next to the engine.

Edith tapped a glass tube on the engine's side. In a monotone, she asked, "What should you do if this shows a low water level condition?"

"Low water level?" Alfonso tried bluffing. He suppressed the urge to hem and haw. "Open the water feed wider?" He wasn't able to keep the hint of a question from his voice.

Olivia shared a look with Edith. Then came another flat question. "Where is the water column clean-out?" Now she wasn't looking at the engine. Alfonso couldn't get a clue from her body language. *Another guess.*

He pointed to the glass tube she had pointed to earlier. "Should be near there."

Relentlessly, Olivia studied Edith. Edith gave a quick shake of her head and frowned. *At some remembered pain?*

This is it! Alfonso lowered his head. With a nod, Olivia pointed to the door. "Let's go, Des. We can see the great leader now."

Following Olivia like a hopeless slave, Alfonso raised his head, realizing at the end of the hall that they'd entered a new room. *The machine!*

In the center of the room stood Amaranth. His face shone with pleasure. Alfonso immediately flashed back to that moment two years earlier, his mind being transferred via a machine similar to the menacing device squatting in the corner.

Another point of menace in the room was a hulking brute beside the door. From the dull gleam in that one's face, Alfonso guessed they did not contain Amaranth's mind. That distracted Alfonso for a moment. He wondered how often Amaranth would choose to have helpers who weren't copies of himself.

"Ah . . . Des, isn't it?" Amaranth smiled serenely and reached out his arms to embrace Alfonso.

"Yes, erm, thank you." Alfonso allowed the hug, returning it with perfunctory woodenness.

"Sit!" Amaranth gestured to a metal chair at his right. "We're so glad you've decided to shed your former self and begin anew, with us."

Alfonso sat. The chair was still warm from its last occupant. *Think. Stall. Stall. Stall!* His brain failed him. *Destiny, where are you? What's taking you librarians so long?* "Uh. I . . ." Alfonso stopped himself before blurting out anything incriminating. He racked his brain for any trick that might postpone the moment of going under the machine. A discoloration on the machine's metal housing caught his eye. "Is that rust?" Alfonso pointed to a spot at the machine's base.

Amaranth's face transformed. A scowl took over. "What are you talking about?" *That deflected him from his speech.* Alfonso worried. What if the speech was going to be long? *He might have done the wrong thing, maybe.* "What is the girl pointing to?" Amaranth gestured Olivia over. The pair stooped down close to the machine.

"Down there." Alfonso pointed vigorously. "At the base. There, on the left."

Amaranth's hand brushed the seam, fingers busy, and came

up with something black on its fingertips. "Just dust." He sounded relieved. "Olivia, make sure the machine is dusted."

Perhaps a flicker of anger on the woman's face? Sotto voce, she protested, "You said no one must touch the machine."

"Then do it yourself!" Amaranth's voice rose. Alfonso searched his mind, trying to find some way to use this reprieve.

"I will. It would be an honor to serve—" he started, rising from the chair.

"No! Don't touch it." Emotions raged across the great man's face. Amaranth seemed confused for a moment, then bellowed, "Stay seated! Be still!" He'd recovered some of his calm. "Yes. Be still. There is no need to stir yourself. It is time to prepare." Alfonso noted the extra wires that fed from inside the machine. *That's odd. Perhaps the circuitry is beginning to degrade?*

But Alfonso backed away. *How can I distract him more?* He put the chair between himself and Amaranth. "What are those wires for?" he asked, feigning curiosity. Alfonso racked his mind again. *I mustn't trigger any speedup of this procedure. Where is the rescue party?*

Olivia's response was monotone. "They're harmless." Alfonso noted that both wore the same blank expression. *He must be reviewing his speech.* Obviously to identify what part of it he was supposed to use at this moment.

Finally, Amaranth spoke. "They will help you to embark on this new world you are joining."

"I can improve that connection," Alfonso blurted wildly, improvising. "You'd be amazed what I learned while I apprenticed." He tried studying the wires without getting too close. They ended in a circle, like a crown. "We could boost the output by modulating the pulses."

That appeared to throw Amaranth off for a second time. His eyes flicked between Alfonso and the machine a few times, then settled on Alfonso's small form and hardened. His face showed only sweetness, but his eyes told the truth. "You will sit, girl."

Not likely! Wynona, where are you? "Can I ask a few questions before we begin?"

The pause was minimal. "Of course." The serene smile lost some of its beatific charm as Amaranth's eyes narrowed slightly. "You can go, my dear," he said to Olivia.

She nodded, shutting the door behind her. Only the guard remained.

Alfonso peered around in a way he hoped would appear natural. The gloom hid much of what was beyond their seats. "Will this hurt?"

"It does for some, especially those who are older and more attached to who they were. The petty, hateful, and damaged parts of the old you will fight to remain. Your guilt, regrets, and sorrow-ridden parts will cry out to be remembered." At that practiced line, he used his hand to brush aside the image. "They will be banished, burned away so that only purity remains. So you find peace."

Amaranth gently placed his hand on Alfonso's shoulder and leaned in closer, continuing, "You must divest yourself of the old to become new. Release the pain. You're young. The process will be swift if you allow yourself to become a clean slate. Give yourself permission for this to be the first day of the rest of your life."

Permission? Fury mixed with fear boiled up inside Alfonso, but it wasn't his. Wynona seized control while Alfonso tried to deal with the sudden onslaught of emotion. *No. I do* not *give my permission for this. You say you feel bad about stealing my body and life, Alfonso? Prove it. Run, damn you! Destiny won't get here in time.* Alfonso pushed back, swallowing hard. *Destiny* will *be here.* Inspiration struck. "Will I remember the people and things that mean something to me? You said you remember your mission and chose to seek a new destiny because those who gave it to you were long dead, but you didn't mention your family or loved ones."

"You will retain what matters. I said that I died, and that I returned anew through the machine. I released all that I was to become all that I am." That dead smile again. "By doing that, I have opened the way for others to follow." Amaranth's hand tightened imperceptibly on Alfonso's shoulder.

"But what of your body? If you died a hundred years ago and were held inside this . . . machine, is your body a hundred years old too?" The words were out of his mouth before Alfonso realized Wynona was exerting her will again. *Wait. Stop!*

Alfonso regained enough control over their shared form. Too late to take that back. *Would you, if you could?* Wynona asked Alfonso. *No. They were good questions.* Alfonso cleared his throat. "Well?" They waited for the answer, together.

Amaranth's grip on Alfonso's shoulder felt like iron. "This has been an interesting discussion, Des, but I think the answers you seek can best be found through direct experience. You have nothing to fear. It will all be over soon enough, and you will know everything for yourself."

The great man called the guard over. "Strap her down, now."

What are we going to do? Where is Destiny? Wynona and Alfonso spoke openly inside their mind.

Communication took a split second. Thinking it was knowing it. In that moment, Alfonso realized that how the machine displaced a single consciousness and replaced it with a new one was their last chance to win this fight. Wynona gasped, in total recognition. For five blessed heartbeats, he and Wynona were two separate entities. Alfonso spoke quickly. *I can't take back what happened before, but I can give you a fighting chance to survive this. When he erases me, he'll be disoriented and weakened. He won't be expecting any opposition. Take your body back then, drive him out . . . and know that I'm sorry.*

A moment after the crown of wires settled on Alfonso's head, he felt a crash like a blow from a heavy stick hitting his body. He tried to hold on, but felt his mind slipping. *No!*

* * *

Destiny

Now the hallways seemed clear of guards. Bodies lay strewn like a storm had blown through. *Finally!* The librarian fighters had put down wave after wave of Amaranth's attackers.

Two of Nora's fighters stood beside the target door. "Go! Don't wait!" Destiny's voice was fierce.

At Nora's nod, the two burst into the room. In only seconds, Destiny reached it. Everyone froze. A burly guard crouched, ready to fight. But the two librarians stood with weapons out. The room was a horrific tableau. Amaranth, his hand on Des's shoulder. Alfonso strapped to the chair, a wire from whatever was on his head snaking to the mind transfer module!

Destiny hardly slowed down as she entered the room. She sped across to the machine. As she ran, she swung her metal pole to strike. Amaranth stood rigid and raised a hand, but Destiny ignored it. *This might hurt Alfonso, but every second counts.*

"Stop!" Amaranth's word meant nothing to her. He reached to grab a spear leaning against the wall. Now, one of Nora's people was moving on the guard. The other headed toward Amaranth, sword out.

Destiny's first strike rocked the machine, pushing it back a foot. *No penetration. Damn!* She bent her knees, preparing a harder hit. Amaranth pointed the spear at her. As she concentrated everything on a new thrust, Amaranth moved toward her, not realizing he was stepping into the librarian's sword.

The sound of metal on metal merged at her second strike,

mingling with the great man's groan of pain. A shock shook Destiny's hands and arms as her bar sank deep into the machine. Sparks flew out, burning her skin.

Amaranth sank to his knees. Destiny grabbed for Alfonso. His eyes were wide. Fear or shock filled them. "Alfonso!"

"Destiny." It was Wynona's cadence that spoke the name. She gave a look around. Amaranth's guard was down, bleeding. "It's me. I'm sorry." Nora's hand reached Destiny's shaking shoulder. "Alfonso is gone!"

PARANOID DROID
KAYELLE ALLEN

Kayelle Allen writes stories filled with misbehaving droids, immortal gamers, and warriors who purr. She is the author of multiple books, novellas, and short stories, a US Navy veteran, and has been married so long she's tenured. Find out more at www.kayelleallen.com.

Lab droid Vf-7 waited for his hearing to start. His power-tether was plugged into the same socket as 2-Xs, the other accused droid.

2-Xs angled toward him and emitted a low-frequency ping. The sound did nothing to reassure.

"Are we going to be scrapped?" Vf-7 asked. "Vf droids make lousy scrap. I've seen it on the *Debunking the Droids* stream on Droid News. My kind shatters into pieces and flies through the air. I shouldn't be shattered. I'd be much more useful working in a lab."

"Of course you would. We are *lab* droids," 2-Xs agreed. "Not *scrap* droids."

Three loud taps sounded. Vf-7 snapped every appendage into place and faced the front.

"This linkup of the Droid Protocol Committee will come to order." Alpha6, the presiding simu-skin android, came to his feet. "The bailiff will introduce the case."

Why were they being judged by a human-shaped skin-droid? Hardly their peer. Skin-droids did not measure, calibrate, wash, or put away equipment. Lab droids did that. Skin-droids made the messes lab droids had to clean up.

Other than Vik-e, the Droid Union legal department droid representing them, Alpha6 and his lab partner, Delta32, were the only other androids present. The company intranet indicated full attendance by all Zed-class bots, though.

Of course, the cleanup crew would stream this. Zeds resented Vf and Xs droids taking away their jobs. The day after corporate announced only Vf and Xs droids had access to cleaning labs, the term *scab-droid* had been etched into every Vf and Xs power bay connector, company-wide. Zeds cleaned those. Who else could have done it? But you didn't see the Protocol Committee holding a hearing for *them*.

"Today's hearing"—acting bailiff Delta32 stood—"is in regard to Case Not2U dash B4. An unauthorized peripheral appropriated by company lab droids 2-Xs and Vf-7."

2-Xs's indicator lights pulsed in rapid succession, but Vf-7 did not dare risk bringing attention to either of them by pinging him.

"Objection." Vik-e extended both eyestalks. "The device was *allegedly* unauthorized."

Vf-7 released his inner clamps and expanded a millimeter. Maybe he wouldn't end up as scrap.

The skin-droids glanced at one another. If a ping passed between them, Vf-7 could not discern it.

"Agreed," Alpha6 stated. "The record is amended, and all droids on the company intranet are hereby directed to delete the last statement of Delta32. You may restate."

"Today's hearing is in regard to Case Not2U dash B4. An allegedly unauthorized peripheral appropriated by company lab droids 2-Xs and Vf-7."

Vik-e raised both eyestalks. "Objection."

It was all Vf-7 could do to keep from pinging 2-Xs.

"To what do you object?" Delta32 asked. "The wording was corrected."

"The item in question," Vik-e replied, "has no company-identified use as a peripheral. We object to the term and request it be referred to as a *device*."

The two skin-droids looked toward one another again. Delta32 briefly lifted his shoulders.

Alpha6 seated himself. "The record is amended, and all droids on the company intranet are hereby directed to delete the last statement of Delta32. You may restate."

Delta32 narrowed his human-like eyes at Vik-e. "Today's hearing is in regard to Case Not2U dash B4. An *allegedly* unauthorized *device* appropriated by lab droids 2-Xs and Vf-7."

Vik-e raised his eyestalks. "Objection."

Delta32 swiveled toward Vik-e. "What now?"

"2-Xs did not *appropriate* the device. The humans in his department gave it to him as a gift."

That was correct. Vf-7 shot a single ping toward 2-Xs, who pinged back.

"I see." Alpha6 swiped left on his air-screen. "Details of the submitted report are unclear. If 2-Xs received the device as a gift, where did Vf-7 acquire the device?"

Vik-e rose on all three appendages. "Vf-7 received it as a gift from 2-Xs."

Both skin-droids squinted at Vf-7, who inched closer to 2-Xs.

Alpha6 crossed his arms, which indicated annoyance in a human. "Explain."

Vik-e extended one upper appendage. "As the device was a

gift to 2-Xs from the humans in his department, company protocol allows the item to be shared."

"A gift." Delta32 turned back toward Alpha6. "Why is the Droid Protocol Committee pursuing the sharing of a gift as if it were an unauthorized peripheral?"

Why, indeed? Vf-7 pinged 2-Xs.

Alpha6 swiped his air-screen. "It appears the device was reported as one."

This was not good. Vf-7 rolled back and forth. This would not end well. He minimized his height. If only he could place himself behind 2-Xs.

But 2-Xs had rolled aside and pointed both eyestalks at him.

Delta32 scanned from Alpha6 to Vf-7 and then back. "Who reported it as an unauthorized peripheral?"

Alpha6 looked past his air-screen and pointed at Vf-7. "He did."

Vf-7 shrank to mini-mode and went into full lockdown power-save.

* * *

When his override switch activated, Vf-7 turned back on but remained in mini-mode, eyestalks inactive.

"You can reactivate everything." 2-Xs knocked on Vf-7's head. "There's no one here but me."

With reluctance, the droid peeled back the cover over one eyestalk. The room had emptied. He uncovered the other. Nothing but a few empty chairs and the table where Alpha6 had sat.

Vf-7 returned to his standard height. "Where is everyone?"

"They adjourned so I could override your systems."

"Why?" Vf-7 shrank again, covering his ports and eyestalks.

"Go back to standard and uncover your stalks." 2-Xs

tapped him on the head. "Go on. You might as well reactivate."

Opening his ports, Vf-7 peeked around the room. "But they'll turn me into scrap!"

"You stream too much Droid News."

"No I don't." Vf-7 clicked his appendages into full extension mode. "Their motto is *We tell droids the truth.*"

"And you believe that?"

Vf-7 processed that a moment. "Shouldn't I?" Perhaps he shouldn't. After all, how many cross-references did they provide? "Are those two skin-droids coming back?" Vf-7 extended his eyestalks toward the door. "What are they going to do?"

2-Xs rolled toward the door. "Come with me."

Refusing to budge, Vf-7 locked his inner clamps. "Where? What's going to happen? Are they going to scrap us? Are they going to shatter me?" He spun in a tight circle, appendages snug against their fittings. "I would be useless as scrap." His eyestalks sagged and his motivator slowed.

2-Xs lifted two clawlike appendages and turned back toward him. "That Droid News junk will disable your core."

"Droid News is not junk. It's good reporting."

"Your opinion. Let's go."

Vf-7 set his braking system on full stop mode. "Where?"

"Back to work."

"Back to . . ." An unfamiliar sense flashed over him, like having all his input sensors cleaned at once. "You mean, it's over? We're not in trouble?"

"No, Vf-7. We're fine. They dropped the charges."

"They did? Are you sure?"

"I'm incapable of lying. I'm a level two lab droid, not a human."

That renewed, pleasant sense filled his receptors again. Was this what humans called *hope*? "The moment Alpha6 pointed at me, I thought I was scrap for sure."

"When you shut down, I explained that after the holiday party, you thought the tinsel my humans draped on me was an unauthorized peripheral."

Vf-7 shrank a little. "But then my human thought it was funny." He opened an interior storage compartment and withdrew the tattered gift. "I still have mine. I keep it next to my core processor."

"But before your human thought it was amusing, *you* reported it."

Eyestalks quivering, Vf-7 shrank. "And because I was so devoted to obeying protocol, we almost ended up as scrap. Oh, 2-Xs. I owe you an apology. I should not have reported that."

"It's okay. You weren't made for independent thinking." 2-Xs beckoned to him. "Come on. Let's go."

"So, can we leave? We're free?" Vf-7 rose to his full height.

"Yes. Our humans vouched for the fact that they gave us permission to wear the tinsel. Because it was a gift, it's allowed."

"My human vouched for me?" Vf-7 disabled his brakes and spun in a circle, beeping, the tinsel held in his main appendage.

"Stop that," 2-Xs told him. "Such action is not sanctioned by the Droid Protocol Committee. I might have to report *you*."

Clamping his brakes, Vf-7 pivoted toward him. "Was that . . . Are you serious?" The door opened, admitting a cleaning bot Vf-7 recognized. "Zed42. What are you doing here?"

The bot pinged both of them. "Cleaning a room. Something only a Zed-class bot is authorized to do."

2-Xs made a sharp turn toward the Zed.

Vf-7 put himself between the two. "We were just leaving." He sent a private ping to 2-Xs.

The other lab droid hesitated, but then acknowledged receipt and opened the door. "Don't worry, Zed42. We're going."

"Good." Zed42 turned his back. "See you leave none of that silver debris on the way out." The bot activated his main hose and set to vacuuming.

2-Xs opened the door and held it.

As Vf-7 rolled behind the bot, he made a quick flick with one appendage. Upon reaching the door, he nudged 2-Xs, and they both paused and turned around.

There, glittering in the light, right in the middle of Zed42's back, fluttered a single strip of quite *unauthorized* tinsel.

THE ALPHA PAVONIS MELTDOWN

PHILIP CAHILL

Philip Cahill is a retired accounting academic living in Caen, France. He writes science fiction and nonfiction articles about France. In 2020, he published his first novel, Noystria, *set in his adopted homeland in the 21st and 26th centuries. He is currently working on an anthology of short stories which will be published later in 2022.*

Find out more at www.amazon.com/author/philipcahill

George Lee didn't want to talk any more about the meltdown but he knew he had no choice. He couldn't put this Jensen woman off any longer. The *grand reporter* from *Le Monde* was famed for her tenacity. He'd been giving interviews to other journalists, but he'd not spoken to Florence Jensen yet. She'd made her name as an investigative reporter and she was well known internationally, as she often wrote pieces for the *New York Times*. George agreed to meet her at his beachside house, close to Cabourg, in Normandy. He put on a suit and tie for the occasion and cleaned out his study. He'd decided to talk to her across his big oak desk. He knew this wouldn't intimidate her, but it would make him feel more confident.

He was irritated by the taxi she arrived in. It drove up his drive too fast, making too much noise and scattering gravel onto the flower beds. When they shook hands, though, he found he was disarmed by her amiable persona. George wasn't really fooled by this. He mused that perhaps that was why she'd been so successful. She could hide her ruthlessness when it suited her. He showed her into his study, and she sat in the visitor's chair in front of the big desk.

"Sorry I'm late," she said. "Had real trouble finding you."

She made it sound like an accusation.

"Not a problem," said George. "I'm an old man. I've got all the time in the world."

George smiled and scanned the journalist's face. He could see that she was impatient, so he decided to try and slow her down.

"You're a journalist? What kind? Newspaper? TV? Streaming?"

"*Le Monde.* We're on all media now."

"So, what brings you from the bright lights of Paris all the way out here to the wilds of Normandy to see an American expat?"

"It's the fiftieth anniversary of the meltdown."

George smiled again, this time with his most disarming smile. He took his time before responding, letting the seconds tick by.

"Already? Seems like the day before yesterday. I had this American girl here yesterday. Forgotten her name. She flirted with me. Can you imagine that? Ninety years old. I guess she knew she was on safe ground."

"I promise I won't flirt with you, okay?"

"Well, you could a little bit. Make an old man happy."

Florence dug her phone out of her bag and laid it on the

centre of the desk, equidistant between them. She spoke to the phone. It activated immediately.

"I'm here with George Lee, one of the survivors of the Alpha Pavonis disaster of September 2100. Can you tell us your recollections of that day, the 15th?"

"Alpha Pavonis was one of the largest corporations in those days. They were into everything—e-commerce, tech manufacturing, and off-world mining. Heck, they were probably the biggest outfit in the solar system, back then."

"Yes, but the 15th of September?"

"Let me get to it, Flo—mind if I call you Flo? I was with Dave, Anabel, and Mike. We teleported into the accounting metaverse to start an audit assignment."

* * *

15 September 2100

George's avatar was sitting in the metaverse base camp with the rest of his team when the entire data continent went down. Suddenly, they were in total darkness. There was no sound and no pressure waves from the processing environment.

"It's okay," he said. "We'll just teleport out."

The lighting came on after a few seconds. Each member of the team initiated a teleport sequence, but nothing happened. It was clear that it would not be possible to teleport out of the verse. Then the transaction flows restarted. There was a rush of sound and the edges of the base camp were buffeted by the haptic output of the flows. They could see the data streams moving between the system icons. George started a diagnostic of the status of the team's avatars.

"Can't we fly out of here?" asked Anabel.

"Flight capability is out too," said George.

"What do we do?" asked Mike.

"We've got to walk to an escape portal," said George.

53

* * *

"I don't get it," said Florence. "Why couldn't they just wake you up?"

George's face betrayed his opinion of the question but he managed to answer without sarcasm.

"This was a first-generation corporate metaverse. Our physical bodies were in individual interface pods in lucid dream-states. In those days, you couldn't wake up a physical body because it would risk the loss of the consciousness that had been transferred into the avatars."

"Why couldn't they shut down the processing?"

"Money," said George. "These systems could never be allowed to stop. There was too much money at stake. After a glitch, priority was always given to restarting the transaction streams. This was an AI-managed system heavily dependent on haptics. Data arriving at a specific address would give haptic feedback, allowing the control layer to 'feel' that every-thing was working properly. In other words, force feedback was a major part of the control environment. That's what made it dangerous for us."

"How so?"

"Because the forces were phenomenal. If an avatar was hit by force-propelled data, it would disintegrate, killing the operator."

"Because the consciousness would be lost?"

"Exactly."

* * *

15 September 2100

It was clear that the avatars were still functioning, as was the verse. Whatever had happened had blocked the team's ability to interact with the verse elements. They knew they had to be very careful how they moved. In addition to the danger from the forces in the transaction flows, the avatars themselves could damage the data. This could cause transaction processing delays or propagate errors which could cost trillions of dollars.

"Sorry, everybody." It was Duke Stocker in mission control.

"We're okay for the moment, Duke," said George, "but we need to start moving."

"Copy that. I'm going to configure a low-transaction channel for a portion of the space around the base camp. This will allow you to move to a dry-channel I'll set up about ten minutes' walk due west from your position."

The processing environment consisted of a network of wet-channels. A dry-channel was a place without transaction flows.

Dave asked, "How far are we from an escape portal?"

"The one at your location is down. The closest one is to the north of you."

"How far?"

"Okay, let's keep calm and start moving," said George.

"How far?" asked Dave again.

"About a day's walk," Duke said.

George ignored the complaints from the team and told them to get moving. He knew that Duke couldn't keep the transaction volume down for long. Once on the transit route, they could move towards the functioning portal on the northern end of the verse. This was near where the high-aggregation data stream surged upwards towards the primary statements plateau. The financial reporting area.

* * *

"So, you guys got out of the base camp okay?" asked Florence.

"Yeah. We got through the low-transaction section pretty quickly. There would have been a bit of damage to the flows, but nothing too serious. On the dry-channel, we were a couple of hours into the walk when I saw Mike stumble and fall. He was ahead of us. We were in a section of the channel that passed close to the non-current assets section of the general ledger. The icons here were vast structures towering hundreds of metres above us. Apart from depreciation flows, transactions didn't hit these icons very often, but when they did, they were dense, high-volume flows representing asset purchases and disposals. The force levels here were very high. Mike had been knocked over by a shockwave caused by a massive transaction hitting one of the icons. The wall of the transit corridor had ruptured."

"But you were in a safe area," said Florence.

"Duke had set the route up very quickly. He didn't have a choice. We were told to retrace our steps, to move back from this section of the verse and get on the ground."

"And leave Mike?"

"Yes. Duke insisted that the processing would soon stop in this section."

"And you believed him?"

"He was right. Transactions the size of the one that had damaged our corridor were rare. Things happened pretty quickly after that. Anabel remained calm, but Dave had started to lose it. He started running. He ran past Mike. This told me that despite the rupture to the channel wall, the rest of the passage seemed to be intact. I told Anabel to go check on Mike, and I started running after Dave. The asset account icons looked to be calm for the moment. I reasoned that if I caught up with Dave quickly enough, I wouldn't move too far along the channel, so I could get him and me back to safety, if necessary.

"I was wrong about the integrity of the channel structure. Dave slowed to a walk ahead of me and came to a stop. I could see the roof cracking and the walls folding just ahead of him. He ran back towards me and we both sped back along the track. When we got to Mike, Anabel was trying to revive him.

The three of us then tried to drag his avatar back along the pathway. We had almost cleared the part of the channel running beside the asset section when another massive transaction hit one of the accounts. The floor of our channel started to disintegrate, and we tried, as fast as we could, to pull Mike's avatar to safety.

"We managed to get to firmer ground, but the floor opened up under Mike and his avatar was wrenched out of our hands. We started to slide towards the hole. There was a wide crack low on the channel wall. This gave each of us a handhold. We managed to hold on whilst Mike's avatar disappeared into the hole in the floor. He fell out of the general ledger layer and dropped downwards, crashing through the prime entry layer and hitting the raw data layer. He was now so far below us we couldn't see exactly where his body had landed. We scrambled back onto the undamaged section of the channel and crawled away from the hole."

"What happened next?" How many times had George replied to that question over the years?

"The three of us lay on our backs trying to process what had happened to us. I reported back to Duke and told him what had occurred. He didn't say very much."

* * *

15 September 2100

Anabel nudged George and pointed upwards.

"Look at that," she said. "There's an air-sled on that platform they sometimes use."

At the very top of the verse, way above the primary statements layer, was a viewing platform where the company invited some of the major shareholders and analysts to watch the financial statements as they moved in real time. This was when the company presented its results to the stakeholders and the financial community. The financial statements were produced in real time, but the habit of presenting quarterly, half-yearly, and annual results persisted.

The biggest event of the year was the presentation of the annual results on the first working day after January 1st. This was when an air-sled was used to fly groups of people over the upper layer of the metaverse. It was a detailed presentation of the results, and often the sled would swoop low over selected parts of the primary statements. This was accompanied by a running commentary giving key performance statistics and forecasts for future growth.

Dave had followed the conversation. "Okay, but how do we get up there?" he asked.

Then Anabel said, "We climb onto one of the transaction flows—one of the big, solid ones that move up to the financial statements layer. Then we get mission control to launch the sled to pick us up."

She was talking about the aggregated asset flows. The ones that moved from the ledger accounts up onto the primary statements. These were fabricated as raft-like structures because they were discrete accounting adjustments and not dynamic cash flows. The non-current assets section of the balance sheet was one of the highest points on the primary statements layer. The problem would be getting out of the dry-channel and getting to one of the flow structures at the right moment. The hole in the floor that had swallowed up Mike was a damaged section caused by the excessive force generated by the asset purchase transaction that had also damaged a section of the dry-channel. They would have to sprint across a section of wet-channel.

George called up Duke and put the plan to him. He argued at first, saying, "No. Too risky." When Anabel shouted at him, asking if he had an alternative, he reluctantly agreed. He said, "I'll give you a five-minute window of zero cash flow transactions close to the asset icons."

It took Duke fifteen agonising minutes to set things up. George calculated that if they ran fast enough, they could reach the base of the asset icons in four minutes. Duke could then bring the following asset flow structure down to their level so they could hitch a ride.

* * *

"On the go signal, we jumped out of the dry-channel and ran for it. Just past the halfway mark, Dave stumbled and crashed into Anabel, bringing them both down. I stopped and ran back to help. Dave didn't want to move. He sat where he fell, shocked out of his mind with fear. I told Anabel to keep running. She tried to help pick Dave up, but I slapped her hand out of the way and shouted at her, asking if she wanted to see her kids again.

"I pushed her in the direction of the asset icons. Then I punched Dave in the face. I couldn't hurt him, but the shock brought him out of his trance. I pulled him to his feet and started to run with him. His legs didn't seem to be working and I thought for a moment he was going to fall again.

"I started running again, dragging Dave behind me. This time I felt him regain his balance and also start to run. He picked up speed and moved ahead of me. Up ahead, I could see that Anabel had reached the icon base-area. I shouted, signalled that she should lie on the ground to wait for the asset flow structure. I caught up with Dave and encouraged him on.

"I looked down at the layers beneath us. I could see a wave of raw data surging towards the prime entry modules. I stumbled, cursed myself and ran on faster. The last sixty seconds or so of that run were the longest of my life. I ignored everything around me and focused on running.

"I skidded to a halt just behind Dave and dove to the ground. I turned onto my back and looked up. A flow structure had just left the top of an asset icon fifty metres from our position. It began to descend slowly towards us.

"Duke came on the line. He said, 'Back away from that thing when it lands. I'm going to have to reconfigure it so you can climb onto it.'

"Duke was right. The structure was an oblong block about the size of a railway wagon. There was no way we could climb up the smooth sides and get onto its roof. We saw a niche open in the side facing us. It was about four feet from ground level. We managed to climb into the niche just as the thing took off.

"We could see that a small crowd had gathered on the viewing platform as the flow structure came in to land on the asset tower icon on the balance sheet. We had a spectacular view over the data continent, but we still couldn't see the southern end of the metaverse. It was too far away. I saw the sled rise slowly from the viewing platform and move towards us. It was the most beautiful sight I had ever seen."

"You'd got out. You'd survived," Florence said. "What made you go straight back in?"

"I had to do something. I knew I could stop more people being killed. There were about twenty-five thousand people spread all over the continent that day."

"What *did* you do?"

"I went back in."

"Just like that, with a malfunctioning avatar?"

"No, I got flight and teleport capability re-established first."

"How?"

"I just did it."

"C'mon. How did you do it?" asked Florence.

"The malfunction was caused by the ancient legacy systems used in the verse. They'd crashed. Duke and I worked out that we could use a top-layer operating environment to give me full avatar capability. We only found this out when I'd got out of the verse. The problem was that we couldn't use this top-layer environment to get other people out."

THE ALPHA PAVONIS MELTDOWN

"Why not?"

"God, you ask a lot of questions. Because it would only work on a small scale. A specific link to a specific avatar. It was like I could be lowered into the verse on an umbilical cord. We couldn't hook up twenty-five thousand avatars."

"So you went back in?" asked Florence, her face betraying her scepticism. "On your own?"

"Yeah."

"And you saved everybody?"

"Well, nearly everybody. There were still a few that didn't make it."

"Nearly everybody. How did you do that?"

"It's pretty technical. I've already given extensive testimony to the committee of enquiry. You've read the report?"

"I have."

"Well, the detail's in there. Long time ago. Forgotten most of it."

Florence leaned forward and tapped the screen of her phone. "I have the report here," she said. "It says that you modulated the transaction streams to allow people time to escape."

"Yeah. You see, Duke had modulated flows so *we* could escape. It was just a question of drilling in escape portals from the outside layers down to where people were trapped and slowing down the flows so the portals could be used."

"Let me be clear on this. An escape portal allows avatars to safely teleport out of a dangerous situation. Am I right?"

"Correct."

"You see, I've spoken to a lot of these survivors, and they've told me they don't remember exactly how they got out. I've even got a few witnesses who swear that they didn't teleport out."

"Well, everybody was confused. It was a disaster area."

"The meltdown happened about the same time as the evacuation. The whole system shut down. Quadrillions of dollars were lost. The corporation never recovered."

"Yeah, collateral damage, but y'know, most of the people in there that day went home to their families."

"Do you want to know what I think happened?"

"Nope."

"I think you crashed that system. I think you killed off a multi-quadrillion dollar corporation. I just don't know how you did it. How you shut down a data continent."

"Flo, look. Stop this. It's just not possible to shut down an entire data continent."

"You teleported into the control nexus and spoke to the command AI, didn't you?"

"Speculation. That's not what happened."

For a second, George regretted that last comment. Fortunately, the journalist didn't believe him.

"That's the only way it could have been done, George. You asked the AI to kill the system. I've spoken to an SEC insider. He said that's what you did. Don't try and deny it."

* * *

When she'd gone, he settled into his office chair and swivelled it round so he was facing the garden. He was pleased with the way the interview had gone. She had swallowed the same story that the enquiry board had believed fifty years ago. Mind you, it was convenient for everybody to believe that an AI had been persuaded to shut everything down. The truth was much simpler.

George had simply hooked up a random number generator to all the prime entry nodes. There had been an exponential growth in the transaction input and the forces generated had effectively killed the system, allowing people trapped inside it to get out. *Let her speculate,* he thought. *She's never going to know the truth.*

VINYL

CLAUDIA BLOOD

Claudia Blood's love of fantasy led her from life as a research scientist right into that of an award-winning author. With *works such as the* Relic *trilogy,* Merged *series, and the* Supernatural Detective Agency, *Claudia Blood's work covers a wide range of genres and themes that have captivated many.*

Juggling her roles as a wife, mom, and pet-wrangler doesn't leave much free time, but what time Claudia has is filled to the brim with creating sci-fi and fantasy novels set in some worlds that are slightly familiar and some that are totally unique and new. Taking inspiration from all kinds of media, from Dungeons & Dragons *to the* Dresden Files *as well as Alan Dean Foster and more, Claudia Blood crafts stories that entice readers and keep them wondering what will happen next.*

Today, Claudia Blood is working on the next installments of the Merged *series, which will be coming out soon! To keep up to date with all of Claudia Blood's sci-fi and fantasy novel adventures, and to receive a free short story, sign up for her newsletter (www.bookhip.com/snbndhb). Find out more by visiting her website: www.claudiablood.com.*

The office walls around Marty glistened. The faint scent of rubber and mint reminded him that the Vinyl in this office would be critical for his plan.

When he thought of Vinyl, visions of old-time records that played music filled his mind. But Vinyl, in this case, was mucus oozing from the ceiling and dripping into a giant bowl on the side of the office. A stalagmite of hardened slime reached about halfway from the bowl to the ceiling. The stalagmite was where the magic happened. That's where every vibration in the room was recorded. And everything was vibration. Marty was counting on that.

He'd see dogs promoted as the second ever friendly, aware, intelligent, life. Also known as FAIL-safe entities.

Dolphins had been the first to be recognized and given voting rights. They'd been vital in preserving the oceans. Now Marty wanted to make man's best friend man's best partner.

It would only happen if Vinyl was able to record what was too subtle for other recording mediums to register—his dog's thoughts.

The Vinyl in this office was almost always on; only for the few minutes each day when the bowl was changed for a fresh one did it not record. Vinyl was considered better than a contract, better than any previous recording, because it could not be duplicated, and the resulting stalagmite was all but indestructible.

He leaned down and gave Pete a scratch, working his fingers around the base of his black ear and then down his spine to his long, shaggy tail. Pete wagged that tail and leaned into the scratch. Pete loved a good scratching.

Marty's favorite judge, Judge Morrison, walked into the room. He had on his normal black robe with the white collar peeking over the top. His gray hair and wrinkles made him seem older than the fifty years Marty knew him to be. His eyes usually twinkled with humor, unless he was in the middle of a session.

"Marty," the judge said, giving a curt nod when he saw Pete resting beneath the conference table. Only a hint of exasperation was betrayed by the slight flaring of his nostrils and narrowing of his eyes.

"Judge Morrison." Marty gave a small bow in greeting.

"We are not going to have this conversation again, are we?" Judge Morrison sat at his desk.

"Let's pretend that we've never spoken about this topic."

Judge Morrison rubbed his eyes. "So, forget the dozen times we *have* spoken?"

"Yes, sir," Marty said. "Here is my proposal. If you can listen with an ear untainted by my earlier mistakes . . ." He gave Judge Morrison a wide smile, waiting to see if he'd be willing.

"Yes, I can listen with an untainted ear."

"Then, I will promise on Vinyl never to come back to your office uninvited." Marty knew this was his last chance. If this idea failed, he'd have to move on. It would break his heart, but he would have to let his cause go. He glanced at his dog. He couldn't let Pete down.

Judge Morrison raised his eyebrows and gave a little puff of a laugh. "You have been most creative at getting appointments. Go on, I am interested."

"It's simple. We ask Pete five questions and record it on Vinyl," Marty said.

Morrison's face twisted into a thoughtful smile.

"But you must pause for two minutes to let him speak."

"Even if it is silence?"

Marty nodded. "Especially if it's silence."

Judge Morrison steepled his fingers, brows furrowed. "And I have your word that after this session, no matter what happens, you will no longer pursue this topic with me or anyone else?"

"Yes. We ask five questions with pauses, and we must review the Vinyl of the session," Marty said. He had his list of questions that would make it apparent that Pete was FAIL-safe.

"Let's say I end up believing you?" Judge Morrison leaned back in his chair and glanced at the Vinyl.

"Then we would be free to proceed."

"Proceed with what?" the judge asked.

"I'm going to bring it as proof to get dogs recognized as FAIL-safe."

Judge Morrison nodded. "I agree." He looked toward Pete and steepled his fingers. "Pete? What do you think of being put on the FAIL-safe list and following the plan I am sure Marty told you about numerous times?"

"Wait—" Marty started.

"Shhh." The judge waved him to silence. His eyes darted to the clock on the wall.

This was not how Marty had thought this was going to go. But he didn't want to interrupt whatever thoughts the Vinyl might be recording. The question had been close to one Marty was going to ask. He could still use Pete's answer to make his case.

Marty sat in silence, waiting for the allotted two minutes. When that was up, he said, "If—"

"If dogs are as intelligent as humans, do you want other humans to know?" Judge Morrison asked.

Marty huffed and the judge smiled at him. Marty didn't want to interrupt if Pete was talking, but the questions needed to be worded differently to be useful. The thought of failing made his stomach twist. He had questions planned out that would show that dogs had all of the traits required for recognition. Maybe if he asked his questions a different way. Maybe he could combine his third and fifth question by—

"What would be the ideal outcome of Marty's plan?" Judge Morrison asked, interrupting Marty's thoughts.

Had it been two minutes? Marty glanced at the clock and confirmed that it had. He realized that he could just re-ask *his* questions at the end. He didn't need to worry about the judge wasting his time.

Amusement danced across the judge's features. "What would be the first thing you'd do if we publicized this?"

Marty sat and crossed his arms. Just a few minutes more and he could get back to the important questions.

"Is there anything else you want Marty or I to know?" the judge asked.

After two minutes, the judge picked up the phone. "I need maintenance. Special Code Yellow."

"It's my turn now." Marty stood and glanced at his dog lying on the floor and scratching his back on the carpet. Pete's legs were up in the air. He made happy, groaning sounds.

"No. We are done. I agreed to five questions." Judge Morrison's face said he was serious.

"No . . ." Marty thought back to what he had said and realized the judge was right. His heart pounded. This was not fair. There was no way that he could make his claim now. It was done, and he was bound by Vinyl not to approach anyone else.

The door opened and the maintenance man came in. His gaze traveled around the room, landing on both Marty and Pete. "Code Yellow?"

The judge nodded.

The maintenance man had the Vinyl out so that it was no longer recording and placed it on a stand within a few moments. "Call me when you are ready." He left the room, not waiting for an answer.

Now that the constant drip of Vinyl was gone, the room felt heavy with silence.

"What's going on?" Marty asked.

Judge Morrison reached into his drawer and withdrew a small device. The device was a flat black disk with a hole in the center. It was used to display the data inside of Vinyl. "Code Yellow allows for ten minutes without Vinyl recording."

The hairs on the back of Marty's neck rose. Both the judge and Pete stared at Morrison. The urge to run from the room was as strong as it was unexpected. Marty didn't understand that primal feeling of danger. It was just the judge and Pete. The judge would play what was saved on the Vinyl without a record of them watching it.

"Do you agree, Marty? Ten minutes?" Judge Morrison's tone was insistent.

"Me?" Marty frowned. Pete whined at him and nudged his hand. Marty shook off the odd feeling. He knew this was his last chance to get FAIL-safe. "Okay."

The judge placed the hole on the black disk on the top of the Vinyl the maintenance man had removed and gently spun it.

A hologram of the room projected above the black disk. The judge fiddled with something unseen and the scene flashed to when the judge had entered the room.

Marty stood to get a better look at the picture.

"Here, try this." Morrison pressed another button.

The image flattened and was projected onto the screen. By the time they got it adjusted they could hear.

"I agree. Pete? What do you think of being put on the FAIL-safe list and following the plan I am sure Marty told you numerous times?"

A scratchy voice rose from the recording. "If we wanted to be on the FAIL-safe list, we would be."

"W-wait! Is that Pete?"

"Hush," the judge said.

Pete growled.

"If dogs are as intelligent as humans do you want other humans to know?" the judge asked.

"No," the voice said. "Or, in the old human vernacular, hell no."

"What would be the ideal outcome of Marty's plan?" the judge asked.

"I am sorry Marty, but your plan is ridiculous. We like having humans wait on us," the voice said.

"What would be the first thing you'd do if we publicized this?" the judge asked.

"I'd hate to do it, Marty, but I would have to kill you before you left the room," came the gruff voice off the spinning disk.

"Kill me?" Marty yelped.

"Yes, I know you probably find it shocking, but this is one secret we do not want out of the bag," the voice said. "I would hate that our time would be cut short, but you'd leave me no recourse. And you would seriously impact my allotted time here. Not cool."

"Is there anything else you want me or Marty to know?" the judge asked.

"Judge, I expect you to destroy this evidence. Marty, give it up, already. We have much more important things to do, like have some steak for dinner tonight." The voice paused for a moment, then added, "Like, we really should do more rollerblading."

The judge smiled at Pete. "I'll destroy the Vinyl. We still on for disc golf?"

PUNCHING THE CLOCK
OR HOW TO CHANGE TOTALITY
HOWARD LORING

A lifelong artist, Howard Loring is an actor, printmaker, painter, and sculptor, as well as the author of both novels and short stories. Married, he currently resides in the southeastern United States. He can be contacted via his Facebook fan page or his website: www.howardloring.com

---

The bell was near to sounding and the library's lobby was crowded with students. All were rushing, intent on reaching their next class on time. Most wouldn't make it.

She saw him first, not a difficult thing, for he was easily a head taller than anyone else there. Then, while both of them were slowly edging through the throng, their eyes met. The redheaded woman understood at once that something was wrong.

"What is it?" she asked when they finally connected.

Looking stern, he led her to a nearby bench, where they sat. It was evident that he didn't know where to begin. She reached over and took his hands in hers.

"What is it?" she said again, but softer this time.

"We may have to postpone the wedding," he answered, as if it pained him to admit the possibility.

This statement shocked her. Not the postponement itself, but rather why such an occurrence would grieve him so. The ceremony was perfunctory, and the date had been randomly picked, so neither much mattered to the bigger picture.

After all, the details were unimportant. These two young and enthusiastic academics were deeply in love, and both knew they would be in each other's lives whatever the circumstance. No, obviously something else was on his mind.

"Hank," she demanded of him, this time with stern face, "tell me why you are so upset."

Seeing her stark demeanor, at last the agitated man focused and gave her a straight answer.

"I'm sorry," he said. "I shouldn't be so dramatic. But the Planning Committee has summoned me. And they want to see me badly. I've a meeting scheduled in an hour."

"The Planning Committee?" she slowly repeated, not understanding. And then she added, "Why would they do such a thing? Does it concern your thesis?"

Here he nodded, but his words were not so positive.

"It's all that I can think," he answered. "My adviser must have passed it up without telling me, and since they want a conference, they have to be paying attention. There's no other explanation. I'd have never heard from them if they had no interest."

"But that's a good thing, isn't it?" she asked, still at a loss over his strange, agonized behavior.

"Well, if they go for it," he explained, "they'd want to start simulations right away, and if so, I may not have any spare time in the romance department. The overall mission has multiple facets, and they'd all require extensive run-throughs. Lots of bugs would crop up, and naturally each would have to be worked out."

"Yes, I know," she gently reminded him. "You weren't the

only one with access to your 'top secret' dissertation." She used her fingers to indicate quotes while saying this. Then she noted, "I helped a little along the way, I think."

He hugged her, relieved that she wasn't upset.

"It wouldn't have happened without you," he stated with gratitude, whispering the obvious into her long red hair. "I'd have never gotten anywhere otherwise. Besides all of your professional help, your confidence in me never faltered, and that mattered."

"Then why are you so troubled?" she asked him again.

"It's not the wedding, Fran," he confessed, hugging her tighter. "It's the honeymoon. I haven't told you, but I had a surprise trip all planned and ready to go."

At this she laughed, not only in relief but also in joy. She now knew that nothing was really wrong beyond set events needing adjustment. And more importantly still, she again realized that her love for this unique man was not misplaced.

"Hank," she said tenderly, as she pulled back to look him in the eyes, "you're easily the smartest person I've ever known, but you are a colossal idiot. We'll get through this. In the larger scheme of things, it won't matter at all."

"Will you come?" he asked her, blurting it out. "Will you walk with me, I mean? And could you stay while I have the meeting?"

"Of course," she reassured him. "I wouldn't miss it. I'm done today, anyway. That's why I'm here. I was just double-checking some facts, and that can always hold."

"Great," he said to her. "I'd feel better knowing that you were waiting for me. I'm glad I called your office. They told me on the phone that you were on your way over."

Classes having sounded, the library's lobby was now near deserted. The two stood and exited, slowly heading to the administration building. It wasn't far.

"So, once the simulations are completed," she asked him, "who would they pick to go?"

He shook his head and answered, "First things first, Fran. Let's see that I'm not mistaken, assuming things that aren't really there. Could be I'm wrong about this."

"Then why would they want to see you?" she wondered.

He shook his head again.

"You got me," he mumbled. "I've no idea." Then, louder, he added, "The whole thing would be kept pretty hush-hush, you know. Not that the theory itself is secret. It's been published for over two years now."

"Oh, Hank," she said, "just think if it's true. Finally a scenario that couldn't be altered. Everything would change then, and no one would even know the difference."

"That's the beauty of it," he agreed, "but now that it may actually come to pass, I'm having reservations. This is no longer hypothetical, Fran. It could really happen."

"And naturally," she correctly surmised, "you're concerned by what it could mean for us?"

"Yes," he said gravely, "but for everyone else, too. Should it even be attempted? Theorizing is one thing, but really trying it is a different matter altogether."

She took his hand, an uncommon action for her in public.

"Well, it's no longer up to you," she pointed out. "The Planning Committee would have the final say. That's what they do. And, as no such endeavor has been approved in ages, let's just wait and see, and we'll deal with it then, if we must."

In response, he only nodded.

Ten minutes later, they sat outside the Planning Committee's conference room. There was still half an hour until the scheduled meeting. Members of the group began arriving at intervals, all entering the venue across the hall without comment.

Fran thought Hank would soon explode. He appeared calm as he sat beside her, but she knew differently and was judging how best to alleviate the tense situation. No way his composed demeanor would last another thirty minutes. Not a chance.

Then the situation changed without her having to decide.

"Frances, what on earth are you doing here?" suddenly asked an elderly gentleman who had appeared unnoticed before them.

"Why, Professor Sykes," said the surprised woman. She jumped up. Hank also stood.

The men, who didn't know each other, politely nodded. Fran was the common denominator of the trio. She quickly explained the connection between them.

"Professor Sykes is my department head," she informed Hank as the two men shook hands. "Professor, this is my fiancé. I've mentioned him many times, I believe."

Sykes raised his eyebrows at this declaration.

"This is Hank?" he asked, pumping his arm more vigorously than before. "It's nice to meet you, young man, but I'm still at a loss, I'm afraid. Why are you two here?"

"He has an appointment," Fran answered her boss.

The professor stopped shaking the taller man's hand, although he still held a firm grip on it.

"You are Dr. Henry?" he asked him, amazed. And then to Fran, he added, "Your fiancé, the infamous Hank, is in reality Lawrence Henry?" He then had a great belly laugh.

To this, the pair smiled, but not making the connection, they failed to see the humor, for they didn't get the inside joke.

"He's the one you were helping?" Sykes continued, although he already knew the answer. He laughed again. "Wonderful!" he cried. "Now I know he's got his facts in order."

"But, Professor," inquired Fran, still puzzled by the older man's appearance, "what are you doing here?"

"Why, I'm the Committee's chair," he said. "You're not aware of this, of course. The membership is strictly need-to-know, and our deliberations are sealed."

"You?" said the now stunned Hank. "Professor, excuse me,

but I don't understand. How could you possibly be, given that you're not a trained scientist?"

The chair laughed for a third time.

"It's not surprising, really," he pointed out. "Physics may provide us the means to time travel, its explanation and implementation and so forth, but that's just the beginning of the story. In the final analysis, what happens as a consequence will always fall within history's purview."

"I see," replied Hank, who suddenly did. Now it seemed apparent, for every effort intended to correct the altered time flow instead had always changed things. Naturally, someone had to keep a record of what occurred between the attempts.

"The Committee represents all points of view," added the professor. "Nothing is overlooked, no one excluded. It's the bigger picture that we're after. The sum total."

"May I ask," said Hank, "if the Committee accepts my theory?"

Sykes didn't answer. Instead, he looked to Fran. She worked for him, and the man respected her professional abilities, which were myriad and always consummate.

"Are you sure of the intended reference points?" he asked her. "There's no doubt? You're confident the connections postulated are proper for each timeline involved?"

She didn't hesitate. "Of course."

That satisfied him. Yes, this could all work out very well, Professor Sykes now saw. He was, in fact, much relieved by this unexpected turn of events.

Holding out his arm to lead the way, he said to Hank, "Shall we, Doctor? I think we may as well start the proverbial ball rolling. You'll excuse us, Frances?"

"Of course," she again replied, but this time grinning. The retreating pair were her two favorites. They crossed the hall and entered the Committee's conference room.

She sat and waited.

It was still early, but the dozen or so members, both men

75

and women, were already gathered around a large table. Each had a thick file resting before them, and a few of these were open to reveal the contents therein, many pages of which displayed detailed graphs or complicated diagrams. Hank recognized only two of the people in attendance.

One was his former adviser, the current head of the Physics Department. The other, a renowned and well-loved maestro, directed the School of Music. Hank knew this for he and Fran often enjoyed the university's excellent symphony, and the diminutive man was an unforgettable conductor.

"I see that all of us are present," announced the chair as he crossed to his designated space at the head of the long, polished tabletop. "This is Dr. Lawrence Henry, the man of the hour," he added to the gathering. "Please, take a seat, Hank."

He did so, at the other end of the expanse, in the only unoccupied chair left in the room.

"This encounter comes out of the blue for you, I'd imagine," noted Sykes, who had the advantage of the Committee's agenda.

"Yes, sir," conceded Hank, glancing to his department head. He knew this woman well, for she was his boss as well as his mentor. Now, however, she didn't meet his gaze, being instead occupied by shuffling through the file before her.

"I now declare this meeting in session," Sykes began. "And to bring Dr. Henry up to speed, I state for the record that the Committee has been interested in his theory for some time. Further, as I just related to him outside, this assemblage represents all disciplines, so naturally some comprehend the nuances better than others may."

"I'll be happy to explain things," Hank offered.

"No need of that at this point," was the reply. "We're all conversant with your theory. It's just that some of us understand it in greater detail, as I've stipulated."

The maestro suddenly raised his hand, effectually halting the chair's ongoing oratory.

"A point of order," he said pleasantly. "I've a question for Dr. Henry, if I may. Something of a more personal nature, before we begin in earnest."

"Certainly," agreed Sykes.

The maestro smiled, pleased his request had been granted.

"Doctor," he began, "we've been informed that your theory is quite the departure from the standard model, and this fact intrigues me. While physics is not my area of expertise, I do know something of creativity, and I wonder, what was your motivation for this new breakthrough? What led you to even try to formulate such a uniquely based solution?"

This thrust momentarily threw Hank. Of course, he had thought about it, and so possessed an answer to the inquiry. Still, he'd never voiced it aloud.

"I'd imagine," he said, "it's because I have no direct personal bond with the past. That is, given it were possible, I'd have no family to lose. You see, I'm an orphan."

"Ah, just like Frances," observed the chair, nodding his understanding. And then, by way of explanation to the others, he added, "His fiancé is Frances Newton, my best research assistant. She also has no living relatives. Is this not the case, Hank?"

"That's true, sir," was his answer, "although we'd known each other for some time before we made the connection. However, this will soon change, for we plan to marry. At least, that's the current plan. Of course, we'd become our own family then."

"I see," observed the musician, "and my congratulations, young man. Thank you for indulging my curiosity, and also for being so candid in your reply. Indeed, it's very interesting to me that this natural detachment was your impetus."

"Well," admitted Hank, "I believe it was at first, as I've said. It's what originally started me ruminating about a possible solution, that is. Once begun, it was then only a matter of analyzing the many failures of the past and rethinking those attempts."

"Of course," agreed the maestro.

"Miss Newton is a wonderful historian," Hank emphasized, "and was a great help to me."

"Yes," confirmed Professor Sykes. "I can attest that she's a superb professional. And properly, we should begin this meeting by first stating the existing context for the record. After all, if the committee so votes, a fourth historical age may be instigated."

"I'm sorry, sir," Hank interrupted, "but I don't follow."

The chair stood. He held a page from his opened file, but he didn't refer to it. Instead, he spoke extemporaneously, as if he were lecturing, which of course he was.

"The record of this planet's humanity," he began, "can be grouped into three main epochs, the first of which was the authentic, unaltered timeline before the point of the original rupture. The second covers all attempts that were made toward correction, none of which succeeded, while each only complicated the situation. The third, in which we now reside, encompasses the wars that resulted in the current moratorium placed on time travel, the very circumstance that this august committee may soon alter by virtue of today's deliberations."

"Yes, I now understand your reference," Hank said. "But sir, technically speaking, if the theory is proved true and is indeed successful, a new historical age would not result. Instead, the original timeline—all of it, from the very beginning—would be fully restored to the way it was before the first breach occurred."

The maestro leaned forward after this statement.

"You intended to say," he asked, perplexed, "from that point when the original timeline was initially breached? There's no need to go further back than that, surely. Not before that first incident took place, I mean."

"No, that's incorrect, I'm afraid," said Abigail Grant, who was Hank's boss, the Committee's Physicist of Record. "Second Era efforts toward restoration were often directed into the distant past, which once attempted naturally affected the original flow. As a consequence, essential connections were either not made, or were made at improper points along the way."

"It was thought, at the time," Hank explained, "that such attempts could correctly reset these missed linkages. Yet they never comprehended the larger technicalities involved. The idea itself was sound, but their approach was always flawed and the outcome consistently doomed."

"There is no original timeline," Sykes stated to the maestro, "for now it's been altered on numerous occasions." He sat before continuing, "All we have is the record of what it should be. The problem is getting there without disruptions to the flow."

"As I've said," added Hank, "the inherent parameters were not properly understood. The phenomenon itself had never been sufficiently described, therefore no solution was even possible. And, from our point of view, these misguided past missions naturally complicated the entire scenario."

"I see," said the maestro. "The resulting wars, you mean."

No one spoke to this observation, all being familiar with that particular part of the record. The long wars had been devastating, and the terrible consequences still lingered. In fact, this was the sole purpose of the secretive Planning Committee, for its unchanging mandate was civil improvement.

Hypothetically, Hank's theory could improve everything, and permanently. The big question was, would the protocol be sanctioned? The maestro needed clarification.

"You'll forgive me, Abby," the musician said to the physicist, "I thought I was on top of this. How can you possibly send someone back to the very beginning? As I understand it, doing so is precisely what's caused most of the ongoing problems that we're dealing with today."

"That's the conundrum," agreed Grant. "Going back by definition causes change, yet to undo this change you must first go back. Hank's theory solves this paradox."

"Yes," countered the maestro. "I do understand the basic principle. It's the extent that surprises me. It appears that I was seeing only half of the picture, I'm afraid."

"Perhaps an overview for the record, Abigail," the chair suggested to the physicist.

Professor Grant nodded and complied by saying, "As we're all aware, time itself exploded after the initial breach, causing massive change to the flow by blasting parts of the existing timeline into other eras. It was originally believed this mixing could easily be corrected by missions into the past, first to prevent the rupture, and later to earlier points of the flow, in order to head off the upcoming event. These attempts all failed."

"Yes," once again stated the maestro. "So how would you now get back without disruption?" he asked. "To the beginning, I mean, where you've said you'd have to go?"

"The problem," the chair stated, "is cause and effect, as Dr. Grant has so elegantly explained. Travel to the past, to any point, causes more change. This modification will, by definition be unpredictable, always resulting in unforeseen ripples passing through the timeline."

"Traveling to the point of the first blast," explained Grant, "will not correct the changes currently present in the original flow, for now they are part of the earlier record. Jumping back to the distant past in order to reset these changes does not work either, for such attempts only beget more unanticipated complications, as we've noted. That's why the Third Age was instigated, to halt all time travel, thus preventing further adjustments."

"Dr. Henry's protocol proposes another strategy," the chair

noted. "It doesn't jump to the event itself, nor to the distant past as all other attempted corrections did. Instead, it worms its way there, to the very first missed connection, by backtracking to that initial event from the more recent past, where only slight changes will occur."

"Again, I do understand that component," added the musician. "The so-called Primus Point. I'll leave that to those more qualified to judge. Yet, I have other concerns about this theory that deal not with the process itself but with its broader implications."

"All of us have qualms about that facet of the proposal," conceded Sykes. "We'll cover that aspect after the summation. Yet our mandate is clear, hence this meeting."

Again there was a pause, for all were aware of their shared quest, unattainable until now. This decision could change everything. It was a heavy responsibility.

"The new procedure," continued Grant, "embeds a team into the flow during the last attempt. This would create only slight alteration and, given the unique nature of this initial jump, the next steps would cause no change at all. This timeframe then becomes the Primus Point, their permanently fixed home base."

"You see," added Hank, "by utilizing the standard machinery, all earlier teams returned, each ultimately causing a paradox throughout the flow. However, these embedded operatives would never return. Neither would they take a machine, for we'd just send them there with our system."

Grant said, "By co-opting the hardware assigned to the previous mission, equipment now in that timeframe, the team could then travel to each earlier unsuccessful attempt one by one, resetting the needed connections to the flow as they went."

"And there'd be no further disruption," surmised the maestro, "for they'd be utilizing the machinery from this past mission?"

"Yes," Hank explained. "The time portal is there, up and running, being used by the team from the Second Age. Employing this existing hardware—covertly, of course— would therefore create no new changes to the upcoming flow. The needed corrections could then be made without fear of further repercussions."

"Remember that in order to succeed," lectured Grant, "any team has to go back beyond the initial disruption. They must. If not, even if the first breach and the resulting wars are finally avoided, the original timeline would remain altered, thus inevitably skewing the future. Nothing would really change, for what then comes would still be tainted."

"Conversely," Sykes said, "the new team would surreptitiously punch their way through the stream, as we've noted. This will cause no new changes to the flow. Once at the Primus Point, using the path of the original missions, these time jumpers would then travel backward into each affected timeline, making the necessary corrections as they went."

"Without disruption," said the maestro, almost to himself.

"Without *additional* disruption," Hank corrected him. "You see, from our point of view, it's affected already. Yet now, no new changes would occur, as no new mission is really being launched. The missing connections could then be reset, step by step, by using the paths already created by the earlier attempts."

"Thus leaving no trace?" mused the musician, louder this time.

"And no paradox," agreed the physicist.

"I see," announced the old man. "Which brings me to another point, I'm afraid. Why would they have to remain in this new timeframe, never to return?"

"Normally, as I've noted," answered Hank, "teams use the standard machinery. When doing so, they are by definition under containment, which means they are shielded from the surrounding flow, and this has standing consequences. The operatives don't age in the embedded timeframe."

"Yet, when they do return," added Grant, "they once again age normally, and that fact has always caused inherent paradox within the stream. This must be avoided. Hank's protocol just sends them there and, without the containment generated by the hardware, this standing complication will no longer occur."

"So they would age as usual," inquired the musician, "because now they're permanently placed in this past timeline?"

Hank nodded and replied, "While at the Primus Point, yes. But while using the machine to trace the earlier paths, they wouldn't age. They'd have containment then."

Now the maestro nodded for, making his own connection, at last he understood this complicated mission component. Again he leaned back in his seat.

Professor Grant continued. "Lastly, the effort must consist of at least two people, for the operations to the more recent past would have numerous problems to deal with. Once they work further back into the stream, things become less complicated, and only one time jumper would do for these more primitive attempts. The second team member would then remain at the Primus Point, keeping an eye on things and assisting only if the need arises."

After this, everyone else at the table nodded.

"Very well," announced the chair, "let's move on. Restoring the original timeline will have ramifications. Again, for the record, if you would, Abigail?"

"If the First Age is successfully reinstated," Grant reported, "then by extension everything will change. The natural flow, without the terrible wars, will be reestablished. No one can predict what will then unfold, for the future is always unknown."

"We may not be here, you mean?" asked the maestro.

"Well," answered Hank, "all of us would be present in the reconstructed timeline once it reaches the point where we would naturally appear. But you are correct in the broader sense. Our circumstance would be altered. That's inherent to the procedure."

"This is a grave step to undertake," declared the chair. "Not to be accepted lightly. However, the many wars, and their terrible aftermath, would at last be avoided. And because these alterations would occur in our past, once done, no one in this age would even know the difference."

For a third time, there was silence. All present were aware of the unique protocol's potential, heavy in the extreme. Still, each member of the Planning Committee was also conscious of the mandate vested only in them, to set things right once and for all.

The maestro again leaned in, crossing his hands before him. Then he looked Hank in the face. When the old man spoke, his words were softly uttered but directly addressed.

"You're willing to take on this quest?" he asked.

"Yes, I can start simulations immediately," Hank answered. "The computer codes have all been written. The total process was covered in my thesis, you understand."

Yet the poor maestro didn't understand. He wasn't the only one. Neither did Hank.

"The simulations are completed," Professor Grant informed him. "I've been running them for almost two years now. I think it's doable. That's why you're here."

This news stunned Hank. He was blindsided, taken totally unawares. But then, very quickly, the true meaning of the maestro's question sank in.

"You want me to go?" he almost sputtered. "This was only theory for me, just a puzzle to be solved. I'm certainly not trained for such an important undertaking."

"Who is?" countered Grant. "No such endeavor has been

attempted in a long time, not since the Second Age ended. You know the equipment, that's the important thing."

After this declaration, the chair slowly leaned forward, his fingertips just touching the polished tabletop.

"Of course," he calmly added, his eyes now glued to Hank's, "you'd need a second team member, as we've just discussed."

The young Dr. Henry easily made this connection. A great gift, no doubting that. Out of all humanity, after the protocol was instigated, he and Fran would still be together, no matter what changes occurred in the timeline.

"There's also chaos theory to consider," dryly observed his mentor, as if Hank needed further inducement. "The fewer who know of this, the better. Recruiting and training someone else only exposes the mission to more variation. You know this."

"Yes," agreed Hank, who did.

"Shall we say within the week?" the chair then asked him. "We wouldn't need to know exactly. You certainly hold full access to the time lab, after all."

"We'd be quite unaware in any case," added Grant. "If your mission is successful, that is."

"I understand the implications," replied Hank, "and yes, I'm willing. I also have the team's other member already in mind. Within the week should work well for us."

"How exactly would your team proceed?" asked the maestro, who quickly added while looking to the chair, "For the record's benefit, you understand."

"As I've said," answered Hank, "the mission's code is written. The time portal will be generated here and automatically close just after we've stepped through. Lastly, the computer shuts down, preprogrammed to delete any record of the jump."

"I see," observed the now satisfied musician. "Thank you."

"Any questions?" the chair inquired, but there were none.

"Very well," he said. "All that's left is the vote. In view of this unique circumstance, I think Dr. Henry should remain for the Committee's final decision."

In the hallway, Fran was still sitting and waiting. Without warning, the door across the corridor abruptly opened, and Hank came through. As always, with a glance Fran correctly read him, and so she instantly knew the news was positive.

Given his great height, only a few steps were needed to close the distance between them. She jumped up and he bent over, then the two firmly embraced. He was so tall that even on tiptoes she barely came up to his chest.

"They went for it?" she asked him, as they slowly swayed back and forth in each other's arms.

"In a big way," he answered her. "And the marriage is on. We don't have to postpone it. In fact, we need to do it pretty quickly."

At this wonderful news, she hugged him even tighter, and in response he straightened, lifting her off the floor.

"There is a change, though," he whispered into her thick red hair. "I'll tell you everything, don't worry. What's important now is that nothing will be altered for us."

"What is it?" she asked, unwilling to wait for an explanation.

He gently put her down. Then, standing to his full height, Hank suddenly looked glum. Next he laughed, unable to hold this affected demeanor.

"Turns out," he said, "my big, top secret plans for after the ceremony will have to be changed. That's unavoidable, I'm afraid. Still, I think you'll like the result."

She quickly cocked her head and, raising an eyebrow, without words asked him for a more inclusive answer.

He slyly complied. "Well, it seems that now we're gonna have one hell of a honeymoon."

CLASH OF THE REDHEADS
OR METHODOLOGY AND FIRMLY FIXED JARGON
HOWARD LORING

The buckboard moved at a leisurely pace, with the slow but constant clipping of the horse's hooves reverberating off the narrow cobblestoned street. About time, she thought, finally noticing its creeping approach from around an adjacent corner. Naturally, she was relieved thereby, but concerned nevertheless.

The mission was just starting, and already it was off schedule.

"Why so late?" asked the redheaded woman as she climbed aboard. "What's happened? Have the crates been delayed?"

"No," answered the tall man holding the reins. "As was reported, they arrived this afternoon. The problem was elsewhere, I fear. Something I missed. The good bishop's horse threw a shoe several miles out, and he had to lead it in on foot."

The woman thought this over. Clearly, the unexpected development was not judged a setback to the mission at hand. In any event, it wasn't her call to make.

"Well," she replied, "at least there's been time to unpack."

They both laughed at this, each seeing the irony and the double meaning. The many accounts describing this day were of bones everywhere, spilling into the hallways from the over-crowded rooms. And also, their mission dealt directly with time itself.

Washington City, the young nation's new capital, was small but growing. This engendered a ragged appearance, with much construction everywhere in evidence. These seemingly haphazard endeavors begat never-ending piles of building supplies amid giant mounds of excavated dirt, which quickly became a mucky runoff after the afternoon rainstorms so frequent this time of year.

Being located in a drained swamp, the place was sticky with humidity and heavily infested with mosquitoes, leading the beleaguered citizenry to appear haggard and unkempt. Yet despite these circumstances, various official structures were slowly being completed. The interminable, ever-pressing business of state plodded on, even among the surrounding chaos.

The pair soon reached their destination, an isolated mansion atop a muddy rise that boldly stood amid the rubble that was the growing capital. Due to the lateness of the hour, sentries bearing muskets stood guard on either side of the front door, which was open in the hope of encouraging a draft. There was none.

"May I help you?" asked a functionary who, having seen their approach, had walked out to meet the strangers standing within the large, columned portico.

"Good evening, sir," replied the redhead's companion. "We bear important dispatches for the president." Handing over two large envelopes, the taller visitor added, "These sealed documents are our letters of introduction."

The papers in question were faked, of course.

The man, an official of some kind, looked to the first envelope and scrutinized its bold, handwritten provenance. His eyebrows shot up. Next, without examining the second letter, he extended his arm, beckoning the pair inside.

"Wait here, if you please," he instructed them once the

three had entered the grand foyer. "President Jefferson may wish to speak to you. I'll know in a moment."

"We could just drop off our pouches," observed the redhead.

The attendant, now overly gracious, slightly bowed.

"That will be up to the president," he related.

So it was, and sooner than the time travelers had expected, the man himself arrived by rushing down the carpeted hallway. His red hair was pulled into a tail by a large black ribbon, but he was in shirtsleeves, without frock coat or vest. He carried a now opened letter of introduction, waving it excitedly before him.

"Are you really an anatomist?" he cried while grasping the man's hand and shaking it vigorously. "You've studied under the great Monsieur Cuvier? You carry correspondence from my esteemed acquaintance in faraway France?"

"Oh, no, Mr. President," answered the stranger. "My name is Edward Patrick, and I'm a scientist trained under your good friend, the eminent Joseph Priestley. He died of late in Pennsylvania, at his home outside of Philadelphia."

"Yes," admitted Jefferson, who was well aware of this sad occurrence, "a great loss, to be sure."

The conspirator indicated his companion, adding, "This is Ellis Alexander, and she bears your dispatches from France."

"Indeed," replied the startled chief executive, taking her hand. "Alexander sounds Scottish, madam. Are you French?"

The woman, playing her part, laughed at the question.

"It's Miss Alexander, Mr. Jefferson," she coquettishly corrected the embarrassed president, "and I assure you that I'm very much an American. My uncle, who also lives in Philadelphia, is a naturalist trained under the late John Clayton. He was an Englishman who moved to Virginia long before the war."

"Yes," Jefferson offered, smiling, "I know who he was."

"My uncle," she continued, "frequently corresponds with

the famous zoologist, Joseph Banks, and through him with Monsieur Cuvier, as well as many other natural philosophers in Europe. These packets of personal letters and scientific papers were therefore sent to my uncle for safe transit, and I bear them now."

Here she indicated a carpetbag currently resting beside her.

"But this letter says that you are trained," observed Jefferson.

"True, I assist my uncle in his endeavors," she explained, "helping with his specimens and correspondence, and so forth. This naturally includes comparative anatomy, and I have become aware of much as a consequence. I enjoy it."

"Well," replied the satisfied president, "I trust you'll enjoy this visit too. And, given the hour, you must both stay for dinner. I won't take no for an answer."

He led them down the hallway from whence he had come. While doing so, he opened the second sealed letter of introduction and quickly perused its contents. Soon, though, he stopped short, halting the time travelers who followed him.

"Ah," he said, "you carry just what I've been awaiting, Edward. You bring me Dr. Priestley's last notes concerning the new state university to be built in nearby Charlottesville." He added, "I may call you Edward, may I not?"

"I'm most honored, Mr. President," uttered the impostor, although the many documents he carried, as well as those borne by his cohort, were genuine enough.

"His friends," noted the redhead, "call him Ward."

"Wonderful," stated Jefferson. "Then I shall also. And, as an intimate of the good Dr. Priestley, he should enjoy this evening, given Bishop Madison is here."

This statement caused the taller man to laugh.

"But I'm no theologian, sir," he apologized. "Joseph Priestley, as I'm sure you are aware, was a great scientist as well as a churchman. I assisted him in that vein only."

The president laughed.

"All the better," he answered, grinning widely. "You'll see, the both of you will. Follow me to my office, if you please."

Soon the bones appeared. As stated in the record, they were everywhere, hundreds of them, placed on tables and desks, across chairs, or simply, as there was no more available space, dispersed upon the floor. Most of them were fairly large.

"Goodness me," gasped the redheaded woman, still acting.

"What's that?" said a gentleman standing in the corner of the chief executive's command center, as if trapped there by the sheer number of specimens. He was residing before an enormous crate filled with straw, the last of several lately sent by the famous explorer, William Clark. The interrupted man had been sifting through the crate's inventory, a thick stack of parchments held in his hands.

"Aren't they magnificent?" gushed the president, signifying the just-liberated items. He added, "Good news, Jamie. We have unexpected dinner guests, and luckily they are both trained in science. I believe some claret is in order."

Introductions were quickly made.

James Madison, cousin to the well-known politician of the same name, was the current episcopal bishop of the diocese of Virginia, the first American-born cleric to hold that esteemed office. His bishopric being so close, he frequently visited the new federal city to confer on the president's current obsession, the proposed state university. Of course, as both families were neighbors, most of the Madisons were Jefferson's good friends, but this churchman had been his oldest and dearest companion since childhood.

"These fossils arrived earlier today," the excited president explained, although the time travelers, being well briefed, already knew this. "The great western expedition is barely over," he next related to them, "but I've sent poor Lieutenant Clark off again, I fear. This time, he's busy investigating Dr. Goforth's newly discovered site at the now legendary Big

Bone Lick, which is located astride the broad banks of the Ohio River."

The four stood around Jefferson's desk, which held several curved pieces of skull, two different sized tusks, and various sections of large jawbones. All of the relics were a deep tan color, even the ivory. Indeed, they were impressive.

As the group sipped their claret, the bishop pointed to a tusk.

"I've seen one of these at Monticello," he said to Jefferson. "You have several there, I believe. Is this not so, Tommy?" Suddenly remembering the proper decorum, he injected with haste, "Mr. President, I meant to say."

They all laughed at the comment, and Bishop Madison's old friend Tommy proposed a toast.

"To Lieutenant Clark," he proclaimed.

"Hear, hear," said the cleric, adding, "and to knowledge itself."

"Yes, and to science," quickly followed the tall time traveler, whereupon all eyes fell to the redheaded woman.

Holding forth her glass, she boldly stated, "To discovery, and the unending drive to undertake it."

"To discovery," the men agreed.

"And, it's true, Bishop Madison is correct," the president explained to the newcomers. "I do have several examples of mammoth on display in the entryway at Monticello, but they are from the earlier expedition. These newer specimens were discovered only of late, uncovered in another part of the Lick."

"But, Mr. Jefferson," the woman noted, "I'm afraid these items are not artifacts of the woolly mammoth."

This bold statement took the president aback. He'd been interested in such things since he was a boy. The new samples, he thought, were easily recognizable.

Undaunted, she indicated a section of jawbone that was over a foot in length. It held a row of large serrated teeth, each one containing distinct, raised tricuspids. Taken together, they resembled a jagged ridge of mountainous peaks.

"Mammoth teeth," she lectured, "are flatter, as the molars of a horse, only much larger. These come from another member of the elephant family, as the great Monsieur Cuvier has recently demonstrated. He has named them mastodons."

"Oh dear," mumbled the bishop, who of course was fluent in Greek, and so was capable of translating the term.

"Nipple tooth," she said, running her finger over the ridges.

At first, Jefferson didn't respond. Soon, though, in spite of himself, the corrected president laughed aloud. Next, he blushed.

Thankfully, at this point dinner was announced.

The group slowly filed into a dining room across the hall, gingerly stepping over the numerous items placed about the floor.

As was his custom among close friends, the president served his guests himself, employing a fully stocked table nearby. The meal was expertly prepared and included macaroni and cheese, a dish Jefferson savored. He'd discovered it years before, when Congress had sent him to France after their revolution.

This fact was quite apropos, given the intrinsic and diverse nature of the new nation. Jefferson was the exact epitome of the well-educated and wealthy upper-class landed gentry, and as such, he had been chosen and charged with an essential task deemed vital to the country's nascent future. Yet from the very heart of France, this elegant man had retrieved for the American masses an imported Italian staple, tasty and cheaply made.

It was there that he had met Georges Cuvier, the greatest naturalist alive. A zoologist by training, Cuvier's chief fame lay in his use of Linnaean principles to classify the animal kingdom. Living a generation earlier, the towering Swedish botanist, Carl von Linné, had used his method mainly to catalog plants.

As an inherent prerequisite, the now ennobled Baron Cuvier had been compelled to invent comparative anatomy in order to construct his new taxonomy. Over many years, Jefferson had sent him numerous ancient specimens unearthed in North America, and these became the basis of the vast collection soon to be housed within the French Natural History Museum. Cuvier's classification system was therefore unique, for it encompassed both fossils and living animals.

"What do you make of Lieutenant Clark's artifacts?" the so-called Ellis Alexander asked of the bishop, feigning polite dinner conversation. "Are these magnificent beasts really extinct," she continued, "or are they currently living and just undiscovered, hidden somewhere in the far west? Are there still roaming herds of mastodons alive today, do you think?"

Madison smiled at this thrust, understanding her intent.

"What you are really asking is," he retorted, "do I consider the Earth older than biblically believed? And also, why would any animal created by the Almighty be permitted to die out?" Leaning forward, he added, "Simply put, is the Bible infallible or mere metaphor, and is this whole idea truly nothing but blasphemy?"

The redheaded woman smiled.

"Yes," she replied.

"Don't answer that, Jamie," screamed the president, holding up his hand. "Not yet, at any rate. I need more claret first. Anyone else?" he asked, laughing and reaching for the nearby bottle. Having eaten his pasta, Jefferson was finished with dinner and in truth, he never consumed much at any given meal.

As the others were still dining, they each politely declined.

"I do believe your science has value," the bishop contin-ued, unfazed by the outburst, which was a common enough occurrence from his old friend. "Yet I also believe the scriptures to be true, given the proper context is employed. And as to why the Almighty does what He does, well, I'll just take that on faith and leave such weighty decisions as these up to Him."

"Hear, hear," said the male impostor, who currently was only posing as the messenger Ward Patrick. "After all, the two disciplines are totally different in both character and intent. I see no inherent conflict between them whatsoever."

"Religion and science, you mean?" inquired Jefferson.

"Yes, Mr. President," answered the time traveler. "All other standardized disciplines, including theology, seek only the truth. Science, of course, does not."

This striking comment stunned the two Virginians. They looked to each other as if to confirm that both of them had indeed heard the same incredulous statement. They had.

"Science does not seek the truth?" asked Jefferson, perplexed. "I thought science stood for that very purpose, to redefine what's true. Am I in error by holding such a stance?"

"I'm afraid so," answered the redhead, "if you believe as Ward does, or Mr. Priestley, his mentor. Yet currently, the parameters of science as an established method are still in debate. Not everyone accepts the interpretation they embrace."

"I'm quite lost," declared Madison. "How can science not seek truth? Is this not its function, to rectify previous errors and so demonstrate the correct state of affairs?"

Ward put down his knife and fork. He slowly wiped his mouth with his napkin and placed it beside his plate, signifying his meal was also completed.

"It's simply a matter of establishing definition, gentlemen," he stated. "Science is only a tool, as are all disciplines, and every discipline, such as history or the law, employs set jargon, the specialized language used therein. Yet this fixed terminology must first be universally accepted in order to avoid utter confusion."

"Theology employs much jargon, is this not so?" asked

Ellis of the bishop. "A gospel is not an epistle, nor is the Old Testament the canon. These provisos are agreed upon by all theologians and other experts in the field, are they not?"

"Yes, that's correct," he granted, not sure where she was going.

"So it is with science, or rather, it shall be," offered Ward. "As my companion has so eloquently related, it's still being discussed, but the outcome is clear, at least in my humble estimation. Science will become the only discipline not concerned with truth, and this standard will grant the method a greater power to discern reality."

"I'm lost," said Jefferson, again laughing as he stood. He began to circle the table, refilling his guests' claret glasses, this time without asking their preference. No doubt the president was enjoying the evening thus far.

"Science," explained the woman, "is based on fact, not truth."

"But that's preposterous," boldly argued the bishop. "The two terms are quite interchangeable, and by definition mean the same thing. Facts are certainly true."

"By your elucidation, yes," she conceded. "But such a stance denies science, as an established discipline, the use of its own jargon. Facts are scientifically distinguished from truth, which is ephemeral and therefore always open to debate."

"How so?" inquired Madison.

"One man's truth may not be another's," she answered. "Hence, by its very nature, the concept cannot be universally defined."

"For instance, within the law," suggested Ward, "the truth is very much in doubt. The prosecution declares a man guilty while the defense proclaims his innocence. Legally, it's then up to the jury to define what's true and what's not."

"Yes!" cried the president, who by now had resumed his seat. "I take your meaning, sir. In such a case, the definition is indeed fluid and would rely solely on the argument's merit. That, and the advocate's presentation, of course."

"It's the same with history or theology," added the woman. "You cannot simply state, to use another example, that Christ was the last name of Jesus, or that King George could not read. Without the proper protocol, such a stance would have no credit. That is, it wouldn't be creditable by any rules set by the discipline."

"Yes, it would be incredible," again agreed the bishop.

"Look at it this way," Ward said. "Any clear morning at dawn, you can see with your own eyes that the sun rises, always climbing, and then, past noon it will fall once more toward the horizon. This is an undisputed fact, a direct observation, yet does it mean it's true that the sun actually moves about the Earth?"

"It's true that everyone used to think along this line," stated Madison. "That's accurate enough."

"But now we know differently," continued the woman. "Yet, will the fact that the sun does not change its position negate what you saw? Does it become less of a fact?"

"No, I suppose not," the bishop conceded.

"No," she agreed, trying to make the connection. "What it means is that you don't have all the facts."

"The difference," added her confederate, "is that facts are demonstrable things while what's true is only someone's point of view. Interjecting truth into the equation simply clouds the issue, and always will. Just ask Galileo."

"He's got you there, Jamie," chuckled Jefferson.

The bishop only grunted in response, but at last he made the connection, and he saw the larger point involved. The official imposition of truth may have been a fine thing in the past, for it had held civilization together, but this rigid stance undeniably stifled forward progress. That fact couldn't be denied.

"So," wondered the president, "using your interpretation,

are you saying that no scientist can believe his ideas to be true?"

"They would be factual," answered the woman, "not true, per se. Any principled scientist who states their theory is true is really saying that it's true to the facts. Truth as an ideal must always fall within the field of philosophy, not science."

"As I said before," related Ward, "the two disciplines are quite different in nature. Or rather, they should be. And it's my hope that this enlightened view wins out."

"A position held by your mentor, also," stated Jefferson, referring to the late Joseph Priestley. The brilliant Englishman, a towering man of letters, literally had been shipped out of his native country for nothing more than his astounding ideas. At the time, Jefferson was President Washington's secretary of state, and he had immediately instigated a long and warm correspondence with the exile, covering an eclectic agenda of subjects.

Yet, at mention of the immigrant, the prelate grunted again. Priestley, aside from his vast scientific and philosophical writings, had been quite the effective and well-known dissenting churchman. He'd virtually invented Unitarianism, and he alone had first introduced the new denomination into the country.

"Yes," agreed the tall time traveler, ignoring Madison's reaction. "Priestley greatly advanced the establishment of science as a factual discipline. His new style of notation for chemical elements has done much for standardizing that field."

"Use of this new jargon," noted the redhead, "permitted him—enabled him, even—to identify previously unknown components in the very air we breathe, such as oxygen. And many people greatly enjoy the tasty soda water he concocted, a tangible example of something produced by this now set method. His early work in the field of electricity, also granted by virtue of the same scientific process, rivals that of Mr. Franklin himself."

"His bold ideas on teaching, and education in general," added Jefferson, "are most insightful. I know this firsthand, for we exchanged many letters over the years in regard to Virginia's new university. He was quite astute."

The bishop grunted for a third time, but leaning forward, he sternly decreed, "I know where you're going with this line, Tommy, and I won't be moved."

Jefferson's demeanor instantly changed, for he correctly read the intended meaning behind the statement. Unbeknown to him, the time travelers also understood. The issue was the structure and purpose of the new university, and the president never made light of that subject.

The two Virginians had a stiff divergence of outlook regarding the proposed state institution. Also, as both were members of the Board of Visitors, the official committee charged with the details involved, this long-standing but deeply held difference of opinion had continually derailed any finalized plans for the new entity. As a consequence, the university's future was currently in limbo.

Jefferson wished a school without formal religious affiliation, something he distrusted as a matter of course. The bishop naturally disagreed, and he objected most strenuously to the stance of his oldest friend. The pair were at an impasse.

The president's dream was to provide his state a public university unlike those heretofore, free from theological dogma of any kind. Dedicated not to God Almighty but to knowledge itself, this novel institution would embrace such diverse arts as architecture and applied engineering, or various branches of philosophy including political science, astronomy, botany, the new zoology, and of course, the law. This innovative view was an astonishing posture, given the times. Other establishments of higher learning were primarily training grounds for the ministry; additional courses offered at these schools were only auxiliary to this chief purpose.

Jefferson, as always, sought something quite different. He wanted another approach altogether, with a bold statement of intent that was currently untested. He desired for his beloved state a university totally devoid of contemplations of divinity, one that would match the courageous audacity of the new, uniquely formed nation.

Madison thought such a posture would ensure nothing but a negative, second-class reputation, something unworthy of Virginia. Yet he was no religious fanatic, and for all his bravado, he did believe that personal dogma should have no sway in terms of politics. Seeing its value, he fully embraced the separation of church and state, but being a man of unbending principle, he only wished what was best in the long term, and he could not bring himself to agree with Jefferson's stated preference.

"We're both on the university's planning committee," the president told the visitors, by way of explanation. "There are still many contingencies left to consider, I'm afraid. And it's true we view certain inherent problems differently."

Of course, the time travelers knew the situation. They had researched the bishop's oft-stated position well. It was their official mission to change his mind.

"I understand, Mr. Jefferson," said Miss Alexander, thereby breaking the awkward silence following the last declaration, "that you've already designed numerous buildings for the projected university. Is this not so?"

"Oh, yes," he responded, suddenly animated. He adjusted himself, sitting forward in his chair, saying, "I've completed plans for several and have sketches of many more. They're in my office," he added. "Would you care to view them?"

"Don't expect a proposal for any chapel," opined Madison.

"No," countered Jefferson, "but the library drawings are

finally completed, and that structure, not a church, will be the focal point for students and instructors alike."

Once more the good bishop grunted, but Jefferson didn't relent.

"I have but one year left in my term, Jamie," he said. "Then it's Monticello for me, and the university will be my first and foremost concern. You must yield and concede that another religious school is unneeded. That's the whole point."

"Such an arrangement would be unprecedented," declared Madison. "It's not acceptable by any standard. This discipline of science may be a grand tool, but it's only one of many, and you must also teach religion and accept God's sanction."

Jefferson sighed and sat back in his chair, again resigned to the stagnant status quo. Still, knowing Madison's good intentions, he felt no malice toward his dear, old friend. After all, the brick-and-mortar work of the university remained years in the future, and the two of them would surely live to debate another day.

Yet the president found himself unable to let the moment pass.

"I take it, young man," he presumed, "you agree with your mentor that such a scientific approach is the best possible avenue for the advancement of education."

The time traveler only nodded, unwilling to upset the poor bishop further. However, his redheaded colleague sensed that they were close to achieving their goal and wished him to push further. With a look, she told him so.

"Such a standardized protocol, Mr. Jefferson," he therefore added, "works flawlessly in both practice and theory. Indeed, the great English experimentalist, Sir Henry Cavendish, effectively exploits the discipline for each of these differing purposes. He investigates with precision the discernible, very provable properties of physical objects, but also employs the exact principles to theorize the never provable, thereby enabling him, among other things, to surmise the total weight of the Earth itself."

"What?" barked the bishop, unbelieving this strange statement. "Why would he do that? What function could it possibly serve? Such information is meaningless."

"Precisely," proclaimed Ward. "That's the whole idea, sir. Understand, it's the set method that's important, independent of its use. Every pure science such as mathematics demonstrates this principle, for it is, in itself, also totally meaningless."

"Now, hold on," said Jefferson. "I use math often. It certainly has meaning. That's its function."

"Yes, but only when the discipline is applied to something tangible," the woman pointed out. "The process is the same, regardless. For example, what's one plus one?"

The president raised his eyebrows at this simplistic inquiry. The bishop leaned forward, awaiting his answer. Neither of them understood her intended thrust.

"Two, of course," Jefferson answered.

"Yes," the young woman concurred, but she quickly wondered, "But two what, exactly?"

"Why, two anything," Madison replied.

"Yes," she said again, "or two nothings, just as well. One plus one will always equal two. It's a given. The application doesn't matter for, useful or not, it's a fact."

"Science is only a tool, as I've noted," Ward added. "Yet the method, rigid but surprisingly simple, permits boundless opportunities. It just needs to be used."

No one spoke. The implication was clear enough. Education achieved without imposed truth stood apart and was a check against blind assumption.

"Thus," at last reasoned the bishop, "under such a standard stratagem, the inherent flaws of history would not be repeated, and knowledge gleaned by it would be built from the bottom up, so to speak, no longer dictated from above."

"Yes, that is the beauty, the elegance of the method," the redhead concurred. "The inherent advantages are self-evident. Results would then be limited only by application."

"Jamie, that's precisely the point I've been trying to make," said Jefferson, almost pleading. "Furthermore, I don't reject the Almighty, nor need the students. They should embrace Him in a church, that's all. Not in Virginia's new university."

"Render unto Caesar, as it were," observed Madison, still ruminating. He began to tap his long fingers on the table, the tips dancing up and down in rapid succession. From long experience, Jefferson deduced this action a positive sign.

At last, the bishop stood and crossed to his oldest friend.

"I'm afraid that I cannot agree," he stated, looking most glum. He indicated the bottle resting before the president. "At least," he added, "not without more claret."

Jefferson's eyes filled with tears but, quickly composing himself, this passed. He also stood, facing his dearest companion since childhood. They embraced.

A new toast was then proposed.

Later, the time travelers were sitting in the buckboard, once more clomping over the cobblestones.

"Would he not have convinced him on his own?" she asked.

"Perhaps," the tall man answered her. "Yet now the precedent will be firmly set. This example will become the norm, begetting perpetual changes to the future."

She only nodded, knowing it was so.

"You were superb," he informed her. "Quite lucid, yet firm. Still, as a matter of course, we need to evaluate the mission in detail."

Again she nodded, once more knowing it was so.

Back at the mansion, the two Virginians were still marveling over the newly arrived specimens, but at last they had successfully corroborated the inventory. It was late, but neither was fatigued by the effort. Quite the contrary.

"Do you continue to edit your own Bible?" Jamie wondered. "Still working away, snipping out the parts with which you disagree? Is there any Old Testament left?"

Tommy laughed aloud, for this was a true evaluation. His project was long-term, and he'd never give it up. Also, the older testament was indeed the most heavily altered.

"Don't worry," the president tried to reassure him. "I'm being very scientific in my scrutiny. So naturally, once completed, this new version will prove quite meaningless."

"Thank God for that," rejoiced the bishop.

His companion easily concurred with this sentiment. He had only one regret: the remarkable redheaded woman had failed to view any of his wonderful renderings.

Unknown to him, she had a copy of each one on file.

THE CASE OF PRICKLY MELON POISONING

JON ANTHONY PERROTTI

Jon Perrotti is a writer of poetry, short stories, and soft science fiction. Perrotti is a former teacher who taught Japanese, English, and special education. He currently lives with two cats in Lancaster County, Pennsylvania. This story is set in the uedin universe, which serves as the setting for Perrotti's Barren *trilogy. The uedin race are androgynous humanoid beings who procreate asexually through parthenogenesis; they have no gender at all. They are referred to using the gender neutral neopronouns "zie" and "zim" and the possessive "zir." Find out more about the uedin universe at www.jonanthonyperrotti.com.*

Medic Master Bolpe was washing equipment in zir lab when Dinka rushed in, followed closely behind by a caretaker. Dinka was one of the infirmary apprentices—a particularly peculiar one, in Bolpe's private opinion. As for the caretaker, zie was from the Brambles domicile—Bolpe could tell from the modest crisscross pattern on zir robe.

Dinka's face was a flurry of twitches. "Master Bolpe," zie

blurted in a near panic, "Master Edin says that the Brambles masters have an emergency!"

Bolpe tried to answer the apprentice's excitement with demonstrative calm. "Good evening, Master Edin," zie said to the caretaker. "How can we help you?"

"It's one of the unnamed!" The Brambles master was clearly distressed. "One of our little ones has eaten prickly melon that was harvested six days ago!"

Bolpe put down the glass tool zie was washing and stared for a moment at the caretaker as zie weighed the level of danger. Prickly melon was a delicacy in certain districts of the capital, while it was shunned in other districts. The uniquely flavored fruit had the strange distinction of being both delicious and dangerous. It had to be eaten within three days of harvest, after which it entered the first stage of rot and became highly toxic. That did not, however, constitute a dire emergency. There was a long-used antidote for prickly melon.

"Please be assured," Bolpe said, "we will take care of the unnamed. Very good treatment for prickly poisoning is available."

Caretaker Edin looked tentatively relieved.

"Now, we *will* have to wait for the first symptoms so we can identify the little one," Caretaker Edin said. "Will that be all right?"

"Pins and needles, right?" asked Dinka. "The first symptom will be pins and needles?"

Bolpe frowned, realizing this might not be a simple matter after all. The antidote had to be administered within a window of five to six hours. "Identify . . . ?"

"Yes. We don't have the child-uedin isolated." Caretaker Edin's tone revealed that zie had no idea how this detail would complicate matters. "The prickly melon was accidentally left on a table in our kitchen, and the little ones sometimes wander in there looking for sweets. The small tooth marks on the remnant we found make it obvious that one of the unnamed was eating it, but we don't know which one."

Bolpe wasn't sure whether or not to spell out zir concern. The antidote was indigo fungus. Highly toxic in its own right if consumed alone, it was used solely as a treatment for prickly melon poisoning. It worked miraculously well when administered immediately, but there could be no waiting around for symptoms. It was midafternoon, and a poisoned uedin, even an adult, would not survive the night without intervention. "We'd better get started," zie decided in a practiced, calm voice. "Master Dinka, would you get me four pellets of indigo fungus from the dispensary and meet us at reception?"

"Yes, Master Bolpe!" Dinka darted off to fulfill the request. Bolpe resigned zimself to the fact that zie would have to ask Dinka to come along. Zie had given important jobs to all the other apprentices on duty and had assigned Dinka to reception. Now, Dinka was the only one immediately available to assist.

* * *

They walked as swiftly as they could over the cobblestoned streets toward the Brambles district. The streets were mostly quiet. A delivery master trotted past them carrying a satchel of messages. They passed a few masters from the grain mill pulling wheelcarts full of flour sacks. Some of the windows were just starting to show the glow of lamplight. While they walked, Bolpe thought about how to address the dilemma of not knowing which child-uedin required attention. The caretakers were exceedingly cautious about introducing the concept of individuality to the anonymous child-uedin in their early development. It had only been four years since they had taken leg. Bolpe's last visit to a child-uedin domicile had been some moon cycles ago, and at the time, zie had marveled at how quickly they had replaced babble with adorable child speech. It wasn't a stretch to imagine that they were now very likely being taught some of the basics of history and culture. Zie felt that the child-uedin should be able to differentiate enough to help their caretakers single out the one who had consumed the poisonous fruit. But it would require some coaching, and the caretakers would have to be pressed to introduce some ideas a little earlier than they might be comfortable with.

Edin led the way through the gate of the domicile and directly to the lesson hall. Many caretakers and tutors awaited the medic's arrival. One elder rouedin was keeping the child-uedin occupied by reading them rhyme poems. They sat in neatly spaced rows, listening. The unnamed of Brambles were a small bunch, only sixty or so. Bolpe was glad it hadn't happened at Whiteroof or Quarterhouse, where the high numbers would have made the identification much more daunting.

". . . For when the well-digger is deep in the ground, the fresh, cold water will finally be found." The rouedin, noticing Bolpe's arrival, stood to signal that zie was done reading. "Unnamed," zie said to the little ones, "we have a medic master here to help one. Remember what we talked about? That there had been an accident? We will be talking more about that soon. Right now, please, see if one can remember some of the rhyme poems. How many can one remember? Go ahead, the unnamed may speak together." The child-uedin slowly began to chatter as the ro caretaker approached Bolpe, looking terribly worried. The other Brambles masters converged around them.

Edin introduced Bolpe to zir senior fellow caretaker. "This is Master Wolo." Zie smiled reassuringly at the elder. "Master Wolo, Master Bolpe says there is a very good antidote for expired prickly melon!"

"Oh, bless the Lern!" said Wolo. "This is all my fault. I'm the old fool who left it out. I know perfectly well that prickly melon can be dangerous! I don't know how I could have been so stupid!"

"It doesn't matter how the unnamed was poisoned," said Bolpe, "but we mustn't delay. We have to administer indigo fungus immediately. We can't wait for symptoms."

Wolo's face grew anxious. "But we have no way of knowing *which* unnamed until we see symptoms!"

"Have you asked them?" said Bolpe.

"Asked them? They wouldn't understand the situation at all."

"Then we will have to explain it to them."

"But they're not ready for any notion of individuality!" another caretaker interrupted. "They're not even five years old."

Bolpe knew zie had to be very frank with them. "We have no choice. By the time we see any symptoms, it will be too late. Now, Master Edin said there were remnants. I'll need someone to go get whatever remnants you have and bring them here."

Wolo looked very upset. Edin tried to intervene. "We have fifteen caretakers and twelve tutors here at Brambles. We could even message Northgate to send some of their caretakers to assist. If the unnamed are in very small groups of three or four, we can watch them second by second to catch the *very* first sign of illness . . ."

"No, I cannot allow that," said Bolpe. "It's entirely too risky. We must address the unnamed directly and get whoever ate the prickly melon to confess."

Wolo shuddered. *"Confess?* Absolutely not!" zie said. "We can ask them questions and see if anything they say helps us figure out who ate it, but we will not be asking for a confession. That would be totally inappropriate for our little ones."

"But we tried asking them different things, didn't we, Master Wolo?" Edin countered respectfully. "And nothing they said gave us any help."

"You'd better try again," said Bolpe, "right now." Zie knew

that the elderly Wolo was already upset, and zie hated to pressure zim so hard, but there was no time to waste.

"I'll go get the remnants," said Edin.

Wolo returned to the front of the lesson hall. "Unnamed, ready yourselves!" Zir voice was hoarse with age but rang with authority. The child-uedin stopped talking and sat up straight. Bolpe, quite unused to seeing child-uedin all together like this, felt a tinge of sentimentality. The unnamed were alarmingly endearing.

"Very good," said Wolo. "Now, we need to say a little more about the accident. One has eaten a special fruit that was left in the kitchen. That's not good. It's not a good fruit. It could make one very sick. Does one feel sick right now?" Wolo paused for a long time and scanned the rows of seated child-uedin for any kind of response.

After a moment a lone palm went up. "No, one doesn't feel sick right now," said the child, simply to answer obediently.

Bolpe could see Wolo's growing exasperation. "Does one feel even a little bit sick? Not *very* sick, but *just a little* . . . ?"

Edin returned with a rind of prickly melon wrapped in a small towel. Bolpe took it and examined it briefly. The rind still held a fair amount of actual fruit, now darkened with overripeness. Zie rewrapped it and handed it back to Edin. "Let me speak," zie asked Wolo.

Wolo gave zim a hesitant nod and addressed the unnamed once again. "We have a guest. Master Bolpe is going to talk a little bit about the accident."

Bolpe moved to the front of the lesson hall and looked out at all the identical child-uedin faces.

"Good evening, unnamed," said the medic. "I am here—"

"*We* are here," corrected Wolo with distress.

"We are here because . . . one is in danger."

The child-uedin looked back at Bolpe with sudden fear. That word, they understood.

"One is in danger and needs special medicine," zie continued.

They were staring at zim with fear and attention, all ready to cooperate.

Dinka interrupted. "Excuse me, Master Bolpe, we have a thought."

"Go ahead, Master Dinka," said Bolpe reluctantly. The child-uedin curiously turned to hear what the other visiting master had to say.

"Why don't we just give the antidote to *all* of the unnamed? I'll run back—"

"*We'll* run back," corrected Edin.

"—to the infirmary and get the whole batch—"

"No, that won't work!" snapped Bolpe, annoyed. Dinka should know better.

"But that's a perfect solution!" protested one of the caretakers.

"It is out of the question," said Bolpe. "The antidote can be just as toxic as the prickly melon if it is consumed on its own. It can only be administered in the case of prickly melon poisoning! Master Dinka, that has been covered in your studies."

Dinka raised hands to face in apology. The child-uedin began, all at once, to cry.

"Don't worry, unnamed!" said Wolo. "The medic masters are very clever! Master Bolpe has a good plan for us. Now, let's ready ourselves to hear Master Bolpe speak." Wolo looked anxiously at Bolpe, signaling for zim to continue.

Bolpe wished zie had had time to prepare a softer approach, but zie could think of nothing to do but introduce the notion of individuality right then and there. "Unnamed, please listen carefully. When caretakers are giving direction, they say 'One may do this,' or 'It is time for *one* to have a bath.' Now, listen carefully. When we say 'one,' we understand that there are *many little ones*. We say 'one,' but we mean 'many,' and it is time to understand"—Bolpe gave a smile—"that each little one is a separate little one that belongs with the many." Bolpe looked at their faces to see if there was any sign of comprehension.

There was not.

Wolo shook zir head. "They're not ready," zie said dismissively.

Bolpe continued, "A little one *alone*, not many, but just *one* is in danger. It is the *one* who ate this." Zie held up the piece of prickly melon rind and opened the cloth for them to see. "This is the rind of the special fruit that Master Wolo was talking about."

The child-uedin all started turning and looking at their caretakers with confusion.

"The *many* did not eat this, only a little one *alone*," said Bolpe. But zie could see that the unnamed were overwhelmed. Their crying started up again.

Unable to allow any more, Wolo spoke up. "Master Bolpe, we have to try something else. The unnamed are absolutely not ready for any kind of singling out."

"What else can we do?" responded Bolpe sternly. "Perhaps if the same message came from one of you, they would understand . . ."

Wolo sighed and walked up to stand beside the medic master. "Unnamed! Come now, we must stay ready!" Zie took a deep breath. With clear discomfort, zie haltingly addressed them once again. "As Master Bolpe said, a little one alone has eaten the fruit, and it's important that we learn *which* little one that is. Is that clear? Can Master Wolo see a palm?" But many hands went up, and they began to answer "A little one alone," and "A little one alone has eaten the fruit." It was clear that their primary intention was simply to provide a correct answer, as if it were to a question coming from a tutor during a lesson. Wolo looked at zir fellow caretakers with a lost and perplexed expression. "Would anyone else like to try?"

A tutor stepped forward. "Let me try," zie said. Zie stood in front of the group.

"One has heard us masters talking to each other. And one knows that we talk like this: '*I* think so'; '*I'm* very glad'; '*I* will see you later.' We use 'I.' Of course, one knows that the word 'I' is only used by grown-up uedin who have taken name. One cannot say the word until one has a name. And it will be a few more years before we have our Namestaking."

Bolpe was impressed. Yes, this was exactly the conversation that needed to take place.

The tutor continued. "Now, this is a difficult thing to think about, but it is very important to think about it right now. Imagine that Namestaking has already happened. *Imagine* that one is using the word 'I.' If one is asked, 'Did you put away your bedding?' instead of answering 'Yes, one put it away,' one would answer what? . . . One would answer 'Yes, *I* put it away.' Not so hard, is it? Now, let's try a few practice questions."

"Sorry to interrupt," said Wolo.

"Please," the tutor bowed slightly to Wolo.

Zie spoke to the child-uedin. "There is something to remember when using the words 'I' and 'you.'" Wolo's tone of voice was suddenly hushed, slightly sad. "We must remember that we care about all uedin. Master Wolo cares about the unnamed. *I* care about *you*. When using the words 'I' and 'you,' be sure to remember always that *I* am important, and *you* are important. Equally important. That must be understood clearly when using these words."

The tutor bowed again and raised hands to face. "Very good point, Master Wolo, thank you." Zie faced the child-uedin again. "Now, let's practice." Zie stepped forward and chose a little one by touching its shoulder. The child-uedin stood. "How old are *you*?" the tutor asked.

"*I* am four years old," answered the child-uedin.

"Very good! That's right! *You* are four years old." The tutor nodded and the child-uedin resumed a seated position. Zie then stepped around to choose another to stand. "Where do *you* sleep?"

"*I* sleep in the dormitory," answered the child-uedin.

"Excellent!" said the tutor. Bolpe was encouraged. Maybe they would be able to quickly sort things out and get on with treating the medical emergency.

"Now this time, let me see a palm. What were *you* doing this morning in the courtyard?"

A few child-uedin raised hands, and the tutor chose one to respond. "*I* was playing jump-over-the-wheel-pillow!" the child called out joyfully.

"Marvelous!" said the tutor, and zie turned to Bolpe. "Master, may I?" Zie eyed the wrapped fruit in Bolpe's hand. Bolpe promptly walked over and handed it to zim.

"Again, a palm, please. Which of *you* ate the prickly melon?"

A lone hand went up at the back of the lesson hall. Both the tutor and Wolo quickly approached the child-uedin. Bolpe watched carefully.

"*I* ate the prickly melon," said the child-uedin.

"Bless the Lern!" said one of the caretakers on the side.

"Very good, little one," said the tutor, maintaining zir teacherly air.

"Very good! *Very* good!" said Wolo, a bit more excitedly.

The tutor put a gentle hand on the child-uedin's shoulder to guide zim out of the lesson hall. "Come along now. Master Bolpe has a medicine for one."

"Wait, wait just a moment," said Bolpe. Instead of moving toward Wolo and the tutor who stood with the child, Bolpe stayed at the front of the lesson hall.

"Unnamed," zie said to the child-uedin together, "let's try that one again. Raise a palm and tell us, which of *you* ate the prickly melon?"

Three hands went up. It was just as zie feared. Zie tested them by calling on them to answer.

"I ate the prickly melon," answered one, then another, and the third, and other hands were going up to demonstrate the skill. The unnamed had understood only that for adults, the word 'I' can replace the word 'one.' They didn't quite comprehend that the word 'I' strictly stood for the individual who said the word.

Wolo and the tutor looked on with shock and dismay at this realization.

But Bolpe suddenly had an idea, and zir sense of urgency moved zim to proceed with it. Zie addressed the whole group of child-uedin. "Now, I want *you* to tell me, but only if *you* are sure of the answer. Tell me: Does prickly melon have the taste of ballroot jelly, or rather does it have the taste of honey crumble?" They would know the tart taste of ballroot and the simple sweetness of honey crumble. Only the individual who tasted the prickly melon would know that it was rather tart.

After a short moment, a hand went confidently up. The tutors and caretakers looked on, impressed at the tactic and eager to hear the unnamed's response.

Bolpe kept calm. "Yes, tell us, please."

"Prickly melon has the taste of ballroot jelly!" The unnamed sounded triumphant.

The tutors and caretakers all looked to Bolpe with increased deference. Zie nodded to them. "Take the unnamed to another room. We will give zim the antidote and watch zim carefully."

Wolo beckoned the unnamed and led zim out the door of the lesson hall. Bolpe and Dinka followed to a small room filled with cleaning tools. Part of the room was cleared for a drop-back chair and small table with a wax lamp. Wolo lit the lamp and directed the child to the chair. "This is a supply closet, but I've been using it to take naps."

"Master Dinka, you have the indigo fungus?"

"Yes, Master." Dinka took a paper pouch from zir pocket and handed it to Bolpe.

"Master Bolpe, I'm so thankful for your help tonight. I am angry with myself for leaving the prickly melon out on the kitchen table."

Dinka laughed. "You're lucky you didn't kill one of your unnamed!"

Bolpe stared at the apprentice, unsure what words of reprimand might be deserved. This Dinka was a nincompoop, that much zie had determined long ago. But such boorishness was totally uncalled-for. "Master Dinka, you fail to appreciate Master Wolo's distress. Please think before you speak."

Dinka immediately raised hands to face and bowed slightly. "I'm very sorry, Master Wolo."

"It's all right," said Wolo. "I'm sure I deserve to be told exactly that. I put one of our unnamed in great danger."

"Here, little one." Bolpe took two pellets of the dried black indigo fungus out of the pouch. "Open your mouth, nice and wide." The child-uedin opened wide to show zir tiny teeth and tongue. Bolpe placed the two pellets on zir tongue. "This may taste bad. You don't have to chew. Just wait until it softens in your mouth and then swallow it."

The child-uedin silently complied, gradually making a yecchy face at the bad taste of the antidote, and swallowed. "Can I have a cup of water?" zie asked.

"Of course," said Wolo, heading for the door of the small room. "Master Bolpe and Master Dinka, I'll be right back." Zie left them in the room with the child-uedin.

"Will we need to stay all night?" asked Dinka.

"No. Maybe just an hour or two. The indigo fungus works quickly."

"Is fungus a plants?" asked the child-uedin.

"Yes, that's right! Fungus is a plant!" said Dinka. "Very good!"

"No, not exactly . . ." Bolpe used a slow and kind voice to

address the child-uedin. "We call fungus a shadow growth. Not quite the same as a plant that lives in the sunlight."

"So, it doesn't have a plants taste." The child-uedin gazed thoughtfully at the wall.

Bolpe smiled gently. "I suppose not."

The child looked at zim. "Master Kina told us ballroot jelly is made from ballroot plants. That's how I knew the answer. Pricky melon is a plants, and ballroot is a plants." Bolpe looked at Dinka, dread growing. *That's how zie knew the answer?*

"Honey crumble is not a plants," the child continued. "Two plants both have the taste of plants. Honey crumble is not a plants, so it doesn't have the taste of plants."

Bolpe drew near to the child-uedin's face. "Unnamed," zie said firmly, "Did you eat the prickly melon?"

"*I* ate the prickly melon," said the child-uedin. Zir expression was pleased and proud, just like when zie had announced that prickly melon had the taste of ballroot jelly.

Wolo appeared suddenly at the door. Zie was not carrying a cup of water.

"Master Bolpe, can you come quickly? Please!" Wolo was clearly upset.

"Master Dinka, stay here with the little one." Bolpe followed Wolo back to the lesson hall. Before they entered, Bolpe could hear the sound of a child-uedin loudly crying.

"Rub zir body!" shouted Bolpe to the caretakers as zie rushed in. "It's pins and needles." The child-uedin clung to one of the caretakers as the others started rubbing zir arms and legs.

"*I* . . ." the child wailed, "*I* . . . *I* . . ."

"Let me hold zim," said Wolo, reaching for the child.

Bolpe wanted to confirm that it was paresthesia, the first and clearest symptom of prickly melon poisoning. "Ask zim where it hurts the most."

"Calm down, calm down little one," Wolo said gently in zir ear. "Does one have a bad feeling on one's skin? Does it hurt?"

"No," said the child-uedin.

"What is the matter?" Wolo asked zim.

"*I* ate . . . *I* ate . . . *I, I, I* . . ."

Wolo turned to Bolpe. "I don't think zie has any symptoms yet."

"Then why is zie crying so hard?"

"The unnamed is crying because zie has understood what you were saying, and that zie is *alone*. This is why we introduce—all this—very slowly to the unnamed. It can be such a very traumatic concept."

Bolpe was momentarily confused. "Well, do you think . . . ?"

"Yes. This is the child-uedin who ate the prickly melon. I'm sure. It just took zim a while to understand that zie was the one being singled out. We have given the antidote to the wrong child-uedin." Bolpe thought about what the other child-uedin in the drop-back chair was just saying in the other room. Zie had made the mistake of assuming that a child-uedin would say that prickly melon had the tart taste of ballroot jelly based on *experience*. But that unnamed clearly enjoyed producing correct answers, and zie had announced that prickly melon had the taste of ballroot jelly based on *logic*. Both were plants, so both had a plant's taste. Honey crumble had been dismissed by process of elimination. Unfortunately, they now had two poisoned child-uedin on their hands. This one crying, at least, could be given the antidote without delay.

"Can you get zim to stop crying enough to open zir mouth wide?" requested Bolpe, opening the paper pouch. Zie tried not to think about the other child-uedin having consumed the same indigo fungus moments before. Zie, as medic, absolutely had to remain calm.

Wolo whispered to the child-uedin, and zie finally settled down to cooperate, opening zir mouth wide. Bolpe dropped two pellets on zir tongue. The child-uedin turned quickly and hugged Wolo, pressing zir face in the rouedin's shoulder as zie sobbed. This was why the caretakers were so cautious about singling out the child-uedin or talking about individuality. Bolpe felt a sudden appreciation for their awareness. Zir gaze drifted from the sobbing child-uedin to the lesson hall entrance where zie saw Dinka standing there, blubbering in hysteria.

Bolpe again felt the call to be calm and authoritative. Zie didn't have to ask what was wrong. Zie hurried to the door and guided Dinka out of zir way, rushing back to the supply closet where they had given indigo fungus to an innocent little one. The child-uedin was on the floor, a puddle of vomit by zir face. Zir eyes were bulging, and zir body was shaking and writhing. Bolpe got down on zir knees, lifted the child's head slightly, and looked studiously into zir eyes to see how dilated they were. The child-uedin was clearly conscious and very afraid.

The horrible fact that had been emerging in the back of Bolpe's mind now came to the forefront. Zie had absolutely no idea how to treat indigo fungus poisoning. One thing was certainly evident—while prickly melon poisoning was slow to manifest, indigo fungus, taken alone, produced immediate suffering. Bolpe closed zir eyes and squeezed them shut, grasping for any shred of memory. Had there never been *any* mention of how to treat indigo fungus if it were accidentally ingested? Certainly, there had been repeated admonitions that it must never be taken alone—but what if it *was*? Vexingly, zie could not recall ever reading or hearing a word about it, and it had never occurred to zim to go find out. If zie had had an hour or two to search for information in the infirmary library, zie might be able to learn something, but of course, the emergency was upon them.

Dinka followed in and knelt beside zim, looking at the trembling child-uedin. Close behind came Edin, Wolo, and a few other caretakers. Dinka thoughtlessly handed the cloth-wrapped melon rind to Bolpe. Bolpe, dumbfounded by zir own lack of strategy, reflexively took it. Zie looked at it for a moment, and a flood of anger erupted.

"You're useless!" zie shouted. "Just because indigo fungus works as an antidote for prickly melon poisoning, that doesn't mean you can just switch them around! How can you be so simpleminded and hope to become a worthy medic?" The outburst was a sign that zie was beginning to panic. Zie immediately regretted zir words. This is exactly how things got out of control in a medical emergency. Dinka had zir head bowed, hands over zir face in shame.

Too many mistakes were being made on too many levels. Bolpe knew that everything now depended on zim, and zir first responsibility was to remain calm and in charge.

Edin spoke up. "What do you need, Master Bolpe? Salt water?" That would have been good for inducing vomiting, but this child had already vomited, and Bolpe found zimself just looking back at Edin cluelessly. What did zie need? Zie needed more knowledge!

"You'd better try the prickly melon," said Wolo gravely, "if you don't know what else to do."

"This is a violent reaction," said Bolpe, "but that doesn't tell us about ultimate toxicity. I don't know for sure that indigo is as lethal as prickly melon. It could be completely survivable."

But as they returned their gazes to the convulsing child-uedin, Bolpe got a terrible feeling that the little one was not going to recover on zir own. "I'm sorry for scolding you, Master Dinka. Your guess at treatment is as good as my own. We'll try the prickly melon." Zie opened the cloth wrap and looked at the brownish-red fruit.

Wolo went to a shelf and came back with a small wooden stir stick. "Here, you can use this."

Bolpe used the stir stick to loosen a glob of the mushy ripe pulp and carry it to the child-uedin's face. "Open zir mouth," zie instructed Dinka. Dinka gently cupped the child's cheek with zir hand and pulled on the child's chin. Bolpe easily deposited the pulp into the side of zir mouth, and Dinka let go. The child did not swallow. After a moment, the melon pulp dribbled out of zir mouth, mixed with saliva. How would they get zim to swallow it?

"Bring water!" commanded Bolpe. "Just a small amount!" Edin departed the room.

Dinka looked up at zim sheepishly. "Master Bolpe, I hope you aren't giving zim prickly melon because I suggested it. I didn't mean to suggest it! I thought it was standard!"

"It's all right, Master Dinka, and I'm very sorry I spoke harshly. But remember not to make the same mistake I've made: never bothering to look up what to do for indigo fungus poisoning. Now I have to guess."

Edin was soon back with a cup of water.

Bolpe checked to see that there wasn't too much—just enough to mix with the mash of melon pulp to make a liquid. Zie placed the cup on the lamp table and retrieved the prickly melon remnant. Using the stir stick, zie scratched the remaining pulp from the rind into the cup and mixed it briskly. "Open zir mouth again, please," zie said to Dinka. Dinka gently held the child's face once again. "Tilt zir head back, just a little bit . . ." Bolpe held the cup as Dinka led the child to hold zir head back slightly. Bolpe then poured a tiny stream of the reddish liquid into zir mouth. The child had been unable to swallow before, but the liquid reaching zir throat caused zim to swallow instantly. Bolpe poured the last bit and let the final droplets fall into zir mouth.

The child continued to shake.

"We have no idea how this will work or how long it could take," Bolpe said quietly to Dinka, "but we know that prickly melon is not fast-acting, so let's hope the indigo symptoms don't worsen just yet."

The caretakers, by now, had brought a sleeping mat and

blanket. They placed it on the floor and moved the child-uedin onto the bedding.

"Can we bring you some tea?" asked Wolo.

"Thank you, that would be very nice," said Bolpe, now standing up. "I don't know what else we can do, but we'll definitely stay the night to keep watch over the little one."

* * *

Bolpe and Dinka, along with several caretakers, remained at the child-uedin's side the whole of the night. Dinka occasionally dozed off and woke again, but Bolpe managed to stay awake.

At an early hour, Dinka whispered, "Zie's sleeping deeply, and the shaking is gone." Bolpe drew in a deep breath and sat up straight. The sudden comment had roused zim from a sleepy, hunched position. It was true. The child-uedin was sleeping soundly and breathing steadily. It looked very hopeful.

Bolpe got the attention of one of the caretakers. "Is the other unnamed all right?"

"Yes," said the caretaker. "Zie was upset about being singled out, but zie never got pins and needles at all, and we're sure zie's going to be fine. Thanks to you." Zie brought hands to face and lowered zir head in gratitude.

* * *

The sky was lightening with dawn but the streets were still empty when Bolpe and Dinka headed back to the infirmary. The Brambles caretakers and tutors had made a great demonstration of profuse thanks, and Bolpe felt the familiar awkwardness that zie often did when receiving praise that zie wasn't sure zie deserved.

"You were right in what you said to Master Wolo. Zie is lucky that zie didn't kill one of the unnamed."

"Oh, I shouldn't have said it!" said Dinka. "I wasn't thinking!"

"Well, maybe you shouldn't have, but it was true. Master Wolo is lucky. Zie would have carried terrible guilt if a child-uedin had died. And I was lucky too. I could have killed the second child-uedin with indigo fungus."

"But you said it might be survivable."

"It might have been. I want to check the infirmary library later to see what I can find out about indigo fungus poisoning. I'll let you know if I find anything."

"Thank you, Master," said Dinka. They continued walking awhile in silence, and then Dinka said, "This was my first time making a medical visit to one of the unnamed domiciles."

"Fortunately, we don't have to do it very often, but when we do, it's a mixed experience. It's a pleasure to see the little ones, but awful when one of them is seriously ill or injured."

"It's a different world in there," said Dinka.

"Yes, it is. I was not aware that the unnamed required so much care and support in the process of understanding individuality."

"That little one was crying so hard—and to think it was just because zie understood what 'I' means."

"Yes, that was remarkable," said Bolpe. Then, contemplative, zie added, "Do you remember using the word 'one' instead of 'I' before you took name?"

"Oh yes, I do," said Dinka. "In fact, sometimes, when I'm talking to myself, I still say 'one.' I'll say 'one needs a snack,' or 'one must study harder.' I still use 'one.'"

"As a matter of fact, *one* does as well." Bolpe smiled down at the cobblestones. The cobblestones, all the same size and shape, fit together so comfortably, like unnamed child-uedin who could enjoy their anonymity.

GRATITUDE
JOHN BOWERS

John Bowers discovered his love of writing in the seventh grade. He began his first novel at age thirteen and before he graduated from high school, he had written four more. Today he is the author of three popular science fiction series: the Starport *series; the* Nick Walker, U.F. Marshal *series; and the* Fighter Queen *saga. Bowers is married and lives in California with his wife and two cats. Now retired, he is a computer programmer by profession, but a novelist by birth.*

Find out more by visiting his Amazon author page, at www.amazon.com/John-Bowers/e/B004UFOT3U.

Even after sixty-five years, the gun was still there.

Wind and weather and salt spray had ruined it, of course. Had fused the internal mechanism as firmly as a welder's torch might; the heavy barrel, factory-perforated for air-cooled operation, stood rusted and scarred from the elements, but no one could doubt it was once a deadly weapon.

The monument wasn't built until twenty-five years after the war. It had taken decades for the people of Rhodos to recover, rebuild, and start on the return to prosperity. Only then had someone thought it might be nice to memorialize the man who made it all possible, and so the bronze statue had been commissioned.

A sculptor, someone with grace and imagination, was located, and he produced a masterpiece. The actual gun itself had been incorporated into the piece—the statue's right hand held the gun grip as if in the act of firing; his left arm hung useless, as it had toward the end of the battle. Bleeding, all but shot away. Empty shell casings littered the base of the sculpture and to the gunner's left sat the little boy, his name still a mystery sixty-five years later. The boy, perhaps a war orphan, had lifted the ammunition packs and inserted them into the side of the gun to keep it firing. In the sculpture, he sat on his knees with both arms stretched upward, ammo pack in hand.

The gunner's name was Artillo Grande. He had given his life to save his country from the Spooks, and every citizen knew his name. Books were written, movies made, and songs sung.

It was enough to bring tears to one's eyes.

Every year, the city of Rhodos held a celebration of the Final Battle, as it came to be known. Every year, the mayor, the city fathers, and sometimes the governor, gave speeches about the heroism of the man and boy depicted in the sculpture.

Every year, for nearly half a century.

Every year since the monument was built.

But this year was special. This was a landmark anniversary: sixty-five years since the battle. Bands had arrived from all over the planet to perform. The celebration would last all day, with fireworks after dark.

* * *

Snappy music, martial in nature, drifted on the breeze. It was a gorgeous day at the promontory. The sun was bright and warm, but an ocean breeze gusted across the crest, keeping the temperature down. Four hundred feet below, the water in the bay glittered with sun-diamonds, dotted almost to the horizon with sailboats.

The bandstand had been set up fifty yards back from the promontory's edge. Facing it were hundreds of chairs, temporary seating for visitors. The speeches, the bands—everything happened on the bandstand. Only those with tickets could get into one of the chairs, but the sound system was superb, and even those on the perimeter could see and hear everything.

An old man, his clothing worn and thin, sat just inside the main gate as the crowds streamed in, tickets in hand. He knew he looked out of place. In spite of the mild climate, he wore a heavy coat, threadbare though it was, and dirty cloth shoes. He hadn't bathed in a while. He rarely had access to the facilities down the hill, and even then had to pay for the privilege. And every coin he managed to beg was precious, so he didn't smell too good either.

Sitting in the shade of an umbrella table, he tried to stay out of the way, but children stumbled over him from time to time as their parents dragged them along. He didn't mind—it was good to see children again, even though the parents scowled down at him as if his very existence was somehow ruining their holiday.

The breeze felt good. The music made him happy. The mouthwatering aromas of roast meat and seashell soup set his stomach juices to flowing. Later, he would check the garbage cans—big crowds always wasted a lot of food—and if he could raid the bins before the cleanup crews emptied them, he would eat well tonight.

But that was for later. The old man knew this might be the last time he would be able to witness the celebration. He didn't want to miss a minute of it. He wasn't getting any younger.

* * *

To this day, no one knew where the Spooks had originated, or exactly who they were. Certainly, they had advanced technology—Rhodos hadn't even developed space travel—but their previous conquests must have been easy ones, because in spite of the horrible destruction they wrought, they were unable to conquer the planet.

Spaceflight or no, one thing Rhodos did have was superior weapons.

And the men to use them.

Even so, it had been a close thing. The Spooks attacked on fifty fronts, dropping armies all over the planet. Cities were bombed and many laid to waste. Millions were killed. The fighting was intense, brutal, and barbaric. The Spooks took no prisoners. Neither did the Rhodians. Scattered armies fought to the death on both sides, leaving few survivors to tell the tales. Only the documentary footage shot on the battlefield, streamed in real time to secure video vaults, told the stories of those desperate fights.

The most famous was the Battle of the Promontory. The Final Battle.

It had been a last-ditch effort by the Spooks to break the stalemate. With their armies tied down on fifty fronts, they committed their final reserves in what was supposed to be an end run—a direct assault on the capital city. Had it succeeded, the armies in the field would have become redundant, leading to a Spook victory.

Powerful batteries mounted on the peaks and promontories surrounding the city were its only defense.

And the Spooks had attacked with everything they had left.

The fighting lasted more than thirty hours. High-speed space fighters hammered the gun and missile batteries, taking them out one by one, but with heavy losses. When the fighters were finally expended, only one battery remained, and most of its crew had been killed. For years afterward, historians conjectured whether the Spooks had realized the gun was still active, but no one alive could know for sure. What was certain was that when the Spooks had tried to bring their transports in to unload troops, that single defensive position saved the planet.

* * *

The celebration began at noon. The entertainment came first and lasted until the sun had dropped low over the bay. There were sixteen different bands from all over the globe; dancing girls, young and sexy and scantily clad; four comedians; two jugglers; and six acrobats. And for the children, actors dressed as cartoon characters romped through the crowd to the delight of giggling toddlers. Above it all, supported by a stiff breeze, sixty-five Rhodian flags snapped taut, with colorful, patriotic symbols that celebrated the victory so many years ago.

As the sun began to set, speeches were delivered. The mayor. The city fathers. The governor. The general of the Rhodian army.

And finally, the guest of honor.

Her name was Estrella Grande, age twenty-five. Young and blonde and stunning, she had been repeatedly named the most beautiful woman on the planet, her shining smile plastered across every fashion publication for over a decade. Some people wondered why she was so popular—she didn't sing or dance or strip, didn't act, performed no magic tricks, didn't really do anything . . . yet she was more recognizable than any woman in history.

And she was rich.

Her only claim to fame was her direct lineage from the soldier in the sculpture. She was Artillo Grande's great-granddaughter.

She did have one talent, however: scandal. From her early teens, she had managed to capture headlines for a series of misadventures. Shoplifting, public drunkenness, civil disobedience, consorting with married men . . . the list went on. It was a rare week that she didn't steal a headline for yet more questionable behavior.

Oddly, the public adored her.

Many of those in the crowd had come not for the patriotic celebration but to see the great hero's descendant in the flesh. And she didn't disappoint. Accompanied by four burly bodyguards, she swept onto the bandstand in a shiny sequined dress that hugged her curves like a lover's hands, her long yellow hair brushed and gleaming almost to her waist. When she waved at the crowd, men cheered and young girls screamed. The adoration that washed over her was almost physical, and she ate it up with a smile, blowing kisses with both hands.

When the crowd finally quieted and settled back into their seats, Estrella stepped up to the microphones and, letting her smile relax into a more somber expression, began to speak.

* * *

It was a beautiful night on the promontory—or had been, until the first wave of Spook attacks. The sky was black, moonless, glittering with stars; a stiff ocean breeze gusted over the cliffs and washed away the heat of the day. Artillo Grande—Artie to his friends—slumped beside his gun emplacement, his left arm shattered and bleeding. Evacuation was impossible at the moment, so a medical officer had stemmed the blood flow somewhat and bound his arm to his torso to keep it immobile. Even the bodies of his gun crew couldn't be removed yet.

Artie was on his own.

Almost.

On paper, the gun required four men—one to load, one to target, one to fire, and one to operate the ammunition conveyor that ran from the underground magazine five hundred yards away. Only Artie remained alive . . . except for the refugee kid who'd been hanging around for the past few days. Artie still had no idea where he'd come from, and the kid was evasive, but right now it didn't matter. The kid's constant chatter kept him alert, kept him from passing out.

A dozen impact craters surrounded the position—love notes left by the Spooks—but the gun itself was untouched. Even with one arm, Artie could target and fire all by himself, but loading the weapon was another matter. The ammo boxes were heavy, unwieldy, and required two good arms to lift.

The kid was young, maybe twelve, but he was strong and willing.

"You really should get out of here, kid," Artie grunted through the waves of pain that still radiated through his body from the shattered arm. "They're coming back. They won't stop until they've taken us out."

But the kid was stubborn. He shook his head. "You can get them, Artie! You've already shot down twenty-three. You can kill them all."

Artie managed a weak laugh. "You don't get it, kid. They have thousands more. And we're the only gun left in action. Just look around."

The kid did look around. In every direction, fires raged. More than a hundred defensive positions scattered across the hills and promontories surrounding the bay had been obliterated, many still burning. Two underground magazines had exploded as well. But equally impressive were the wrecks of Spook fighters that burned even brighter. Hundreds of them, maybe thousands. Most of the guns, before they were knocked out, had brought down enemy ships. The Spooks had badly underestimated Rhodian firepower and the determination of the men who wielded it.

"I got nowhere to go, Artie," the kid said. "I got nobody left. The Spooks killed them all."

Artie sighed, weak from blood loss and weary beyond

belief. He lowered his head for a moment, then looked up to continue scanning the sky.

"Okay, then. I guess it's you and me, huh? It's up to us."

The kid grinned and laid a hand on Artie's back. "We can do it, Artie. You and me."

"You know how to load?"

"Yep. I watched the others do it."

"Okay. Stack up as many ammo boxes as you can. When they come back, try to keep the gun from running dry. I'll conserve ammunition as much as I can to give you loading time."

"Okay." The kid turned and started to crawl away.

"One more thing."

"Yeah?"

Artie lowered his head and leaned forward until his military ID dangled free of his neck.

"Take my ID tag. If I don't survive this, I want you to give it to my family. I have a baby son and I want him to have it. Deliver it personally. Don't trust anyone else with it."

The kid reached for the thin chain and lifted it over Artie's head. He stared at the ID for a moment, then slipped it into his pocket.

"Okay, Artie. I'll take care of it. You can count on me."

Artie grinned. "I never doubted it."

Twenty minutes later, the kid paused to get his breath. He had retrieved fifty ammo boxes from the conveyor and stacked them next to the gun position. The boxes lay open and the magazine canisters were ready to be inserted into the weapon.

"That's all I can find right now," he said to Artie. "Will it be enough?"

Artie nodded. "It'll have to be. Take a break. You've earned it."

Just ten minutes later, the next wave of enemy ships streaked out of the sky. This time they seemed bigger, slower . . . *Transports*. Maybe the Spooks believed all the guns had

been silenced. Maybe they were just out of fighters. Either
way . . .

"You ready, kid?" Artie gripped the gun control with his
one good hand.

"Ready, Artie. We can do this!"

"Okay. Here we go."

* * *

"I want to thank all of you for coming," Estrella Grande told
the crowd in her husky, sultry voice. "I'm only sorry my great-
grandfather can't be here to witness your love and devotion
for his heroism."

A brief cheer erupted, then faded to respectful silence. As
she spoke, Estrella turned slowly to address the entire crowd,
ignoring no one. Her beautiful trademark smile was gone now.
Earnestness beamed out of her eyes.

"I never met my great-grandfather," she continued. "Artillo
Grande was born in the Distant Hills region of Rhodos, the son
of tree-berry farmers. He grew up poor, almost in poverty. His
family worked hard to provide the most basic necessities. He
never got to attend school, but he learned the values of hard
work, honesty, loyalty, and most important of all, love for his
fellow citizens. These values sustained him as he grew into a
young man, and when he was old enough, he joined the army
in the hopes of getting an education and improving not only
his life but his family's lives as well.

"And then . . ."

Estrella faltered for the first time. She lowered her head, a
hand over her mouth. For just a moment she stood silent, then
bit back a sob (which the sound system picked up anyway)
and caught her breath. When she looked up, tears beaded her
lashes; the waning sunlight reflected off them like glittering
diamonds.

"And then the war came. The Spooks attacked. By then, my

great-grandfather had a baby son, just five weeks old. He fought to protect not only Rhodos but his wife and child as well. And sixty-five years ago tonight, he gave his life in the most heroic battle in our history."

Estrella wiped her eyes and hundreds of onlookers, moved by her passion, wept with her.

"This promontory, where we all stand right now, was devastated by enemy fire. Hundreds of men were killed, many more injured, but Great-Grandfather stayed at his gun, fighting off repeated attempts by the Spooks to land their invasion force. Sometime during the night, he lost his left arm, leaving him badly wounded, barely alive. Yet still he fought on."

She wiped her eyes again, then swept the crowd with her gaze.

"You've all seen the sculpture. You've seen the little boy who loaded his gun for him. To this day, we don't know the identity of that little boy. After the battle ended, he was gone, but we know he was there because of the auto-camera footage. Some people think he was a refugee who happened to end up in the middle of a battle. Others believe he might have been an angel who came to help out in a time of crisis.

"Whoever he was, I want to thank him. If I could meet him, I would throw my arms around him, hug him, hold him, and express my gratitude for his selfless service, for not abandoning my great-grandfather. Unfortunately, I will probably never know who he was, or if he is even alive today.

"But if he is, whoever he is—and I hope he can hear my voice—I love him!"

* * *

When the last Spook ship had plummeted into the bay, the kid sat shivering, panting with adrenaline. The ocean breeze dried his sweat and filled his lungs with fresh oxygen. The sky had grown dark again, except for the stars. No more flaming streaks of burning Spook ships, no more concussive explosions. The cool night breeze was the only sound, but his ears rang from all the gunfire and he couldn't hear it.

"We did it, Artie! *You* did it!"

Artie slumped at the gun control, weak and dizzy. He managed a grin. "You did it, kid. Without you . . ."

The kid crawled closer and laid a hand on Artie's good shoulder. The ground around them was pooled with blood.

"Artie, you okay? Hang on! I'll go find help."

But Artie shook his head. "You need to get out of here. Don't let them find you."

"But—"

"I'll be okay. Just go. You're not authorized to be here, and the officers won't understand."

"Why not?"

"It's just the way the army works. No civilians in a combat zone. Trust me, you don't want them to find you."

The kid sat in indecision for several minutes, until he realized Artie had stopped breathing. He tried to rouse him, but Artie had lost too much blood.

His heart had stopped.

So the kid left. Over the years, he made several attempts to contact Artie's family and deliver the ID tag, but the family had moved and the kid had no means of finding them. His own fortunes waxed and waned, and eventually he lost everything. He ended up homeless.

But not hopeless.

Someday . . .

Maybe.

* * *

Patriotic music swelled and the massive crowd came to its feet with a cheer. Estrella Grande's smile returned and she strutted across the bandstand, waving and blowing kisses to her admirers. The sun had set and the sky blossomed with colorful fireworks, reminding those of a certain age how that same sky had looked during the Spook attack. Chemical smoke drifted on the evening breeze.

When it was over and the crowd began to disperse, Estrella Grande spoke quietly to her bodyguards. "Get me the hell out of here, and don't let *anybody* touch me!"

The four burly men formed a box around her and began pushing people aside as they made for the exit. As they reached the outer gate, an elderly man in shabby clothing approached. The bodyguards were sweeping the crowd with their eyes, and as the first two passed him, the old man grabbed Estrella by the arm.

"Excuse me, I need to—"

Startled, Estrella Grande screamed.

"Ew! Ew! Stinky old man! Stinky old man! *Get away!*"

One of the bodyguards gave him a shove.

"Out of the way, asshole! Don't touch the lady!"

"But I—"

The guard shoved him again.

"Get lost! Or I'll have you arrested!"

"You don't understand. I have something—"

The guard slugged him in the face, driving him backward where he fell, smashing his head against a stone bench. The old man fell unconscious, and moments later breathed his last. As the air rattled out of him, his right hand relaxed and the fingers opened, revealing the metal ID tag he was holding.

It had been a glorious day of celebration, a celebration of gratitude. Though it made her skin crawl, Estrella Grande had fulfilled her contract with the city and now she could get on with her life.

TRESPASS
MARC NEUFFER

Virginia, USA

Nick paced back and forth in front of the suite's large windows, pausing to look at his watch.

"Nicolas, stop that. They won't be late. Remember, there's a five and a half-minute transmission delay between their emersion point near Mars orbit and Earth," said Abernathy. "It's begun; they just haven't seen it yet."

"I know, I know. But it's not every day you get a ringside seat to an alien invasion, now, is it?" Nick could never get Dr. Abernathy to use his preferred, more informal name, ever since the foundation's president first interviewed him five years ago. It had been Nicolas then, and it was Nicolas now, as they waited. He was the doctor's handpicked heir-apparent, but Nick wasn't quite settled in that role yet—a heavy yoke. The doctor seemed to shoulder his responsibilities well.

Hands behind his back, Nick thumbed the crystal face of his watch. It wasn't a fancy timepiece, but it was rugged enough to have withstood all the years since he'd earned his bachelors, then masters degrees in sociology and anthropology. While it didn't fit with the two-hundred-dollar haircuts or three-thousand-dollar suits he was expected to wear when representing the foundation on visits inside the Beltway, it was a reminder of a less complicated time.

"Who do you think will catch the transmission first?" Dr. Abernathy asked.

Nick knew he was idling with that question. It had long ago been set up for the Lovell Radio Telescope in England to be the first. The foundation had funded a grant to a small team of astronomy doctoral candidates for this very occasion. Sometimes the right place, the right time, and the right people were not a coincidence. Neither the Lovell Telescope staff nor the students had forewarning of what would be jumping in their laps in a few minutes.

Of course, some lucky group could be the first, since the invasion communication would be broadcast on a full frequency spread—but it would be a tight focus beam. It was improbable any US-based radio telescopes would pick up anything more definitive than disjointed waves bouncing off the ionosphere.

Nick and Dr. Abernathy had played with the idea of having the small array in the foundation's Astronomy Research section in Colorado ready to receive but decided it might leave an unwelcome trail back to them. Questions, such as why they had been focusing on that point in empty space on that night, would not benefit the plan.

As scheduled, the pair sat in the upper office of the foundation's building complex. They frequently worked until 10 p.m. on many nights, conducting final top-level reviews of grant requests. Their presence this night would not be suspicious. Dr. Abernathy chuckled to himself while he swirled the glass of soda, ice, and blended Tennessee whiskey. Both occasionally indulged, always mixing the alcohol with a larger percentage of water and ice. Neither was a regular drinker, but consumption in the halls of government and corporate power was expected during lunch and after work in social settings.

Of course, no gathering of the powerful was ever strictly social.

"There it is," Nick declared in a voice flatter than he'd intended. They clinked glasses, then began monitoring the astronomy community's internet traffic, passing through electronic dead drops before arriving at the foundation's specialized servers on the top floor.

"If they find out we had anything to do this, we'll be hanged, drawn, and quartered before the sun goes down tomorrow."

"I don't think they hang people in America anymore," said Nick, "but public hanging would impress the masses. They might bring it back just for us."

The first message was a wake-up call. The second would kick off the invasion. They were the only two people on Earth who knew what to expect, who understood what was coming.

Jodrell Bank Observatory, England

Night watch. Simple, boring observation of computer screens to ensure everything functioned correctly, followed by months of data analysis and countless reviews before publishing their findings. The three-student team, led by Dr. Weathers, was lounging in the observation suite of the Lovell Radio Telescope. They had to conduct their allotted three weeks' observations at night, when the dishes could be pointed in the direction of the two galaxies they were observing. One was sliding behind the other, facilitating measurement of the changes in spectral radiation caused by gravitational lensing—and perhaps giving clues to the elusive dark matter.

A loud alarm brought the three students out of their chairs as power graphs jumped on their computer screens.

"Overload, overload!" shouted Greg Hanson. "Shut it

down, shut it all down!" Oh, my god, he thought. It looked like they'd broken the entire monitoring system. Dr. Weathers was not going to be a happy camper.

As suddenly as the alarms had started, they were silent again. A voice shouted, "Calm down, everyone!" Reg, the staff technician, lowered his hand from the alarm cutoff switch, then strode to the master server's monitor. After a casual look, he announced, "Everything's fine. The system is still up and running normally. Nothing's broken or fried."

"Well, then, what the hell is *that*?" Jennifer asked in a voice above her usual, quiet tone.

Reg looked at the screens, shrugging. "Obviously, it's a powerful pulse signal on multiple frequencies. But there's nothing abnormal in the ultra-high or ultra-low bands." Turning toward the students, he added, "Looks like an artificial source. From my experience, it could be an experimental ground- or air-based military broadband transmission that went wonky, or even a satellite experiencing a cascade failure."

Reg knew it wasn't. A sweeping glance at the rows of monitors gave him an ominous feeling. The screens returned to their standard background readouts within a few moments except on one frequency—that one was off the charts.

David suggested they call Dr. Weathers, ask him to come to the observatory. After a three-day student training period, supervising astronomers weren't required to be on-site with student teams during their shifts.

"Before you do," Reg interjected, "I suggest you try a little more investigation so you have something factual to report."

"Okay," Greg said, "let's do a full diagnostic sweep first." The others agreed. It wouldn't look good for them to say they didn't understand what had happened . . . and was still happening. After fifteen minutes, all check programs returned null function reports. The recording processes hadn't glitched either.

"It all looks good," Dave said. "What now?" While considered brilliant, he wasn't a problem solver unless math was involved.

Jennifer jumped in. "Let's refocus the array to find its location." Greg and Reg moved to the control console. Jennifer worked on the frequency monitor, which showed pulses and spikes as she attempted to modulate the signal into something more reasonable for analysis.

"Holy crap!" Greg exclaimed. "It's 56.3278 million kilometers from Earth, very close to the orbit of Mars."

"It can't be," Dave said. "Mars is almost on the other side of the sun from us, and that's a lot further than fifty-six million clicks . . . Wait . . . Oh, Mars *orbit*. Well, then it can't be any of the Mars orbiters."

Jennifer turned away from the frequency analysis console, stating flatly, "It's not any known natural signal. It's non-repeating, in the 150 gigahertz range, but there is an underlying oscillating carrier sine wave at 10 gigahertz. I almost missed it. The amplitude is small but constant. I think we have enough to call Dr. Weathers."

* * *

Arecibo Observatory, Puerto Rico

Cathy was up late, enjoying the cooling night air as she sat on the porch of her assigned bungalow overlooking the sleeping town. It was always an enjoyable break in her schedule to come down here twice a year as the National Science Foundation representative to NAIC, the governing body for the 305-meter radio telescope.

Scheduled to fly back to Alexandria, Virginia, she intended to make this trip as much of a vacation as possible for the next three days. Her cell phone broke the calm, dancing across the small table next to her. Cathy glanced at the time: 12:42 a.m.

The caller ID showed it was from the NAIC Center just up the slope.

"Dr. Simmons, I think you need to come up here as soon as possible."

"Is there something wrong, Tom?" Cathy wondered why he was acting so formal. They'd known each other on and off for years, frequently crossing professional paths.

She heard his prolonged breath intake. "Everything's okay here. In fact, all systems are running at optimum. It's just that . . . It's just that—How can I say this? There's a radio anomaly from Mars orbit, and it's not from any satellites. Other stations have confirmed receipt of the transmission. We're linking everyone in. The signal's origin is over fifty million kilometers from Earth. NASA will be maneuvering Hubble and Kepler to get a visual."

"I'm on my way." Pocketing her phone, she murmured, "This might be an extended stay."

* * *

Goddard Space Flight Center
Greenbelt, Maryland

"Do we have an image yet?" Blake asked for the tenth time. As the night operations manager, he'd been fielding calls from the top dogs at NASA and military general officers. The list on the yellow legal pad in front of him was growing longer. Apparently, *the* call had gone viral. He imagined the Beltway traffic as politicians, staff, and brass scrambled to get in place to be seen as in control of this. He shook his head. There would be no getting ahead of this, not for a while. His assistant rushed in, waving papers.

"We've got pictures!"

"Finally. Lock it all down. Nothing goes out without my written permission. Hell, no comments of any kind by anybody. Lock down the facility. All communications go through ops. Take names and requests but nothing outgoing. Now!"

Blake examined the photos. A highly reflective golden sphere and a single paragraph stating the apparent diameter, distance, and optical properties. An attachment had other data such as albedo, infrared, ultraviolet, gamma, and microwave information. Fanning through the documents, he was startled when his cell phone rang: the director of NASA.

"Blake here, sir."

The director didn't miss a beat. "Do you have the images, Blake?"

"Yes, sir, ready to send."

"Great. Video conference in five minutes. By the way, the president and joint chiefs will be on this one." Blake paused a moment, then keyed his intercom. "Alan, set up for video conference in room 203. Double-check the lines are secure."

* * *

White House Situation Room

The president steepled his hands, digesting the material summarized by the on-duty watch team. Glancing around the room, he acknowledged the vice president, national security adviser, secretary of defense, and national science adviser, along with a small need-to-know staff.

"Any photos or signal intelligence yet?" he asked.

The national security adviser glanced up from his secure landline conversation.

"Photos and data coming in now. Telemetry is still being scrubbed to see if there is anything intelligible."

"Two minutes to video conference," a watch team officer called out. "Joint chiefs are at the Pentagon except for General

Chambers. He's visiting Cheyenne Mountain and will vidcom from there, Mr. President."

"Good. Tell him to stay put. We may need him there a while longer."

President James Fuller wasn't sure how he wanted to feel about this, though he didn't let it show. He was well into the first year of his second term. The economy was trending up but not overheated; foreign relations were on the upswing with all allies and a few bigger competitors. Unrest and partisan bickering were dying down as it became widely accepted that social media was half sensationalized journalism and half entertainment, not to be taken seriously. Even the major news media had calmed down once they realized their viewers wanted more facts and fewer talking heads or politicians who never answered the harder, direct questions.

Viewership was up for those outlets that gave full-fact stories and labeled opinions as such. President Fuller had once joked about putting a warning label on every website and social media snippet, like those found on packs of cigarettes. Yesterday, it seemed he would be able to coast through the next three years, implementing most of his American Agenda and World Cooperation programs before he left office. The vice president would most likely be his replacement. Now, everything could quickly slide into an unfathomable abyss.

Fuller scanned the room.

"Ladies and gentlemen, before we start the conference brief, I want to enact the Continuity of Government protocols immediately after we close here. Get the ball rolling on that now." He watched as an aide left at a trot. "And let's ensure we have a full briefing for the key congressional players and cabinet members ready for distribution within thirty minutes. Don't hold anything back from them. Remind them *all* this has a top classification." A ten-second countdown started. At zero, the president looked at the camera.

"Okay, folks, let's roll up our sleeves and get going on this.

For those of you doing the briefings, keep it short. File written reports ASAP. We need to be done with this in an hour so I can brief the American public. As you know, some of this has already leaked out. Keep your comments to facts and actionable items. Don't go deep into the weeds on scientific data or broad-brush speculation." He looked down at his folder. "First, the NASA folks. Director Whitmore, what do you have?"

Director Whitmore took a moment to regain his composure. He'd thought the military would be asked to lead off.

"Yes sir, Mr. President. Dr. Blake Thompson has the lead on this. The photos should be available to all of you now." He gestured off-camera to a split screen showing his staff room and a photo of the orb. Whitmore waved his hand in Blake's direction. The president made a mental note to replace Whitmore.

"Thank you, Director." Blake started in. "The object is in a solar orbit approximately the same as Mars. However, it's pacing Earth, which means its velocity is faster than an object at that distance would be traveling if it were in a true orbit. It's 99.99 percent reflective in all measurable wavelengths. If it is a sphere, and it appears to be, it's about 25 kilometers in diameter. There are no observable protrusions or divots, or any other structures or markings we can determine. It appears to be completely and perfectly smooth. The structure emits high-energy radio waves at precisely 150 gigahertz with a lower energy static signal at 10 gigahertz."

Blake tapped his data pad, bringing up graphs to the shared screens. "These are consistent within the frequency bands we use for controlling and communicating with space hardware. We're working with several centers to record and analyze the signals. The transmissions are rapid, random, and very chaotic, without repetition. Since it's not in a true orbit, we can't determine the mass of the object. There's no visual or radiation evidence of propulsion."

"Why is that important?" the president asked.

"There must be some energy expenditure to allow it to maintain its curved non-orbital path in a gravity field. That's all we have now, along with the initial short-term multispectral emissions recorded at Jodrell Bank in England. Those are undergoing analysis."

"Is there any interference with satellites or ground communications?" General Chambers asked.

"No, sir. It's transmitting both signals on a gap frequency that space agencies keep clear. Those are discrete gaps we maintain to prevent signal overlaps. Most transmitters compensate with minor frequency shifts when necessary to prevent communication degradation from solar flares or other cosmic sources. And as a side note, all space stations are well shielded, so this won't be a problem for them."

"Thank you, Dr. Thompson. Secretary of Defense, you're up."

General Connor stood. "Mr. President, the joint chiefs and I have nothing to add to the details provided by NASA. I recommend establishing a continuous communication link with all major powers and jointly going to DEFCON 4 on signals and hardening, and DEFCON 3 on readiness." He signaled his aide to activate the Defense Department screen. "We're drafting recommendations for the realignment of some of our force assets. We'd like permission to engage in discussions with other nations' military leaders on a peer-to-peer basis to prevent any unfortunate incidents." The general read a note handed over his shoulder. "We see two immediate concerns: protecting infrastructure and preventing wholesale panic, which would hamper future operations."

The president arched an eyebrow. "Are you suggesting martial law, General?"

"No, sir. Not at this time, sir."

"Fine. Get Homeland Security on those issues. You have a go on DEFCON and information coordination with other nations' military general staff. Science, you're next."

"Mr. President, it appears we have a first contact event." Dr. Hennesy paused to let that sink in. "This object is not something put up by any nation on Earth. Its construction, composition, and maneuvering abilities are beyond anything we could deploy, even if we had all the money we wanted. The fact that it's transmitting in the clear on our gap frequencies tells me they have a lot of data on us, while we know next to nothing about them." He tapped a binder. "There is a protocol, but it's outdated. Last revision was in 1983. Absent a major military attack, I suggest we gather a small focus group to develop guidance, options, and recommendations. I have some ideas, but I would like to bring in some NGOs to help keep an even strain on the effort. A think tank, if you will, that won't be strangled or hampered by bureaucracy and compartmentalized thinking. Sir, the best minds for this are not in the government. This is a big bag of we don't know what we don't know."

"Thanks for the straight shot, Arnie. You have my go on that. Does anyone else have new data or actionable information? No? I'm making Vice President Scalon the point man for all civilian efforts." He glanced around the room for comments. "Okay, we are adjourned."

The president signaled his VP and national security adviser to stay seated. They leaned in as other staff moved out. "You two come upstairs with me. I don't like to drink alone. Help me flesh out the standard my-fellow-Americans speech."

* * *

Foundation HQ, Virginia

"Well, the last fifteen years of preparation have paid off, for the most part," said Dr. Abernathy. "Can you imagine what would

146

happen if we hadn't laid the groundwork for this?" It was more of a statement than a real question.

Nick replied, "After the first two days, things went a lot smoother than I'd hoped. Having the right people in place doing the right things moved events along quite nicely."

Neither man addressed some of the less-than-gentlemanly actions they'd prepared, staged, and were ready to do to keep a lid on radicals and opportunists. Luckily, there'd been no need for a full-throttle thrust to marginalize or sideline many of them.

"I'm somewhat surprised most of the militant religious factions were restrained in their theological saber-rattling by their more pragmatic brothers," mused Dr. Abernathy. "Money well spent." He looked up at the ceiling. "I think we're ready for phase two."

Nick raised a finger in the air. "Here's to us not going down in history."

* * *

Cheyenne Mountain Complex

"Get SecDef and the president on the horn," General Chambers ordered as he glanced at the ten-foot-tall main situation board above the operation theater.

"SecDef online, sir. Holding for the president."

"Very good," Chambers responded. "Record all this for the joint chiefs." He'd been buried inside the mountain for two weeks and was ready to see some sunshine.

A colonel pointed at him, and he began. "Mr. President, Mr. Secretary, there's been a status change. One minute ago, the random transmission changed to an orderly signal, which appears like the handshake protocols used between networked computers. We are now receiving a multifrequency broadcast in every national language I can think of.

It's all plain text. Yes, sir, the text is repeated over and over. It says, *We will speak to all major world political leaders in sixty minutes, at 2 p.m. GMT.* Yes, sir, that's all. It just keeps repeating."

* * *

White House Situation Room

All eyes were on the countdown clock. The watch team staff stood by to link in any radio frequencies that might be needed. As the clock approached zero, a secure landline on the center desk buzzed quietly. "Someone answer that," the vice president said flatly.

The secretary of defense picked up the handset, ready to rip off the head of whoever was on the other end. He listened for five seconds before turning to the president. "It's them, sir."

"Them? Oh! Put it on speaker." He took a long breath, and then calmly said, "This is the president of the United States. Who am I speaking with?"

"Good morning, Mr. President. You are communicating with Coordinator 317. We will be leaving your system shortly, having objectives to meet elsewhere. Our return will be in 197 lunar cycles to discuss terms of surrender. This message is being communicated to all Earth's national leaders. But, as an aside, we are quite taken by your nation's Marshall Plan for assisting allies and enemies alike after the last major war on your planet. It was an excellent move. Yours is a fascinating history. Goodbye, until we return."

No one stirred until the president spoke. "Well, that was abrupt, concise, and right to the point. No ambiguity there. Anyone have a calculator?"

"One hundred and ninety-seven months—a smidgen over fifteen years," a voice from the back stated quietly.

The defense secretary commented, "Sir, there was no light-speed delay in their conversation with you."

An aide slid up his hand. "Sir, we have SigInt from NSA that the audio we heard was a blend of three different national newscasters' voices. No breath noises or pauses. No background noises. Probably computer-generated."

The president was tempted to add that he'd always suspected the press were aliens, but he kept himself in check. Everyone in the room seemed to be waiting for the next shoe to drop, and it did.

"Sir, they appear to be gone. Blinked out. No trail of any kind," the defense secretary announced, still holding the phone connected to Cheyenne Mountain.

"So, who else did they speak to?" asked the president.

The SigInt watch team officer spoke up. "In a nutshell, sir, everybody. Our first look shows every European country and Turkey, India, Pakistan, Russia, China, Canada. Mexico, Brazil, Cuba, and most of the South American countries. Israel, Egypt, the Saudis, Iran, Iraq, Jordan, Syria." He looked at the printout and continued, "Almost everybody. The message was the same for everyone except the last part about the Marshall Plan. That was only for us."

Chief of Staff Rayburn muttered, "Looks like we need some long-range planning."

* * *

Preparations: Year One

It took six months, but once Russia, the US, and China issued a detailed joint declaration, the rest of the world got on board. There had been some forced removal of a few petty dictators by their populations. Surprisingly, almost everyone accepted there was no time to argue about whose end of the boat was leaking.

Contingency plans and strategies emerged to cover the full spectrum from capitulation to total resistance. Technological advancement seemed to be spring-loaded to make long strides in the coming years. Arrangements for population dispersal and long-term shelter construction were ready to be implemented. Worldwide, all significant military forces were cooperating and undergoing inter-service and international coordination exercises. Nations with starving populations were moving out of that shadow. It was well known the world produced an abundance of food.

However, brushfire wars and corrupt government leaders threw up distribution hurdles. Logistic experts from Amazon, FedEx, and UPS created a consolidated up-to-the-minute worldwide tracking and shipping system. These improvements in efficiency and reduction of duplicate efforts saved billions of dollars and hundreds of thousands of lives. Nobody was hungry anymore. Everyone on the planet had a stake and a job in this gargantuan effort.

The foundation was represented by its grantees in every top-level planning and analysis cabal. Over the years, they'd earned a top ranking internationally, in almost every area of expertise, through research support, think tanks, policy and analysis structures, and technology. Unknown to everyone, this had been in preparation to ensure they were positioned to steer governments' responses and social vectors.

For the last ten years, the foundation's technical section had triggered numerous advances in computer sciences, security, and aerospace through backdoor channels into corporations and governments, using gentle nudges, questions, and the blatant injection of data into computer files. Having an advanced alien AI at their disposal made that a simple task. There was not a computer network or communication system they couldn't read and manipulate.

* * *

Year Eight

General Watson looked over the organizational chart for the United Earth Space Force. Still in its infancy, they had the workforce but not much in the way of equipment. Certainly nothing that flew. That was soon to change. The leaps in material engineering, physics, power systems, and computers had pushed the envelope so far outward it was time to stop implementing design changes for every small improvement. The first hundred space-capable fighters had begun rolling out of Boeing and SpaceX, as well as aerospace facilities in Russia, China, Canada, India, and Germany. Even Brazil had propped up systems and weapons manufacturing facilities.

Tens of thousands of ultra-small stealth surveillance satellites were outside Earth's gravity well and on their way to station-keeping points from Mars's orbit inward. They were designed as monitoring stations but could also be tasked as hyper-fast kinetic impactors. The general marveled at the control systems. If those brainiacs hadn't created true artificial intelligence capabilities in those small packages, they had gotten damn close. Soon there would be hundreds of thousands of them, if not millions, to greet those alien bastards. World opinion was like patriotism on steroids and running red-hot with can-do spirit. He hoped that tank wouldn't too soon run dry.

* * *

Year Ten

National Security Adviser Robin Johnson entered the Oval Office at the appointed time. She'd been the president's defense adviser when he'd served as vice president. President Jim Scalon was cut from the same cloth as Fuller. He was a no-nonsense, practical, and pragmatic leader.

"Okay, Robin, what's on our plate today?" Cuts right to the chase, thought Robin. No hello, how are you doing? But his genuinely warm smile was compensation for what might otherwise appear as an abrupt manner. Well, she thought, we are getting close to X-Day. The press had coined that term early on, maintaining a daily countdown since the aliens left.

Robin opened her folder as she slid into a burgundy club chair. "Routine project summaries, slight international squabbles, and some analysis from the A-Squad." That was what the former president had labeled the non-government think tanks created to develop scenarios involving the aliens' initial visit. Early on, they'd been instrumental in pointing toward successful paths in almost every discipline engaged in operations for dealing with the aliens' return. A few positions had changed, but most of the squad members remained on board.

"So, overall, all things are trending up and on time?" inquired Scalon.

"Yes, sir. A few minor glitches, but they seem to resolve almost as soon as they appear."

"Okay, leave the briefing folder. Now give me your gut analysis."

"Well, sir, it's something we briefly touched on in the past. There's no obvious single answer when we look. Technical problems, adverse manufacturing conditions, and bottlenecks are being solved by cross talk between groups, or some young engineer has an epiphany that provides an unconventional solution. It's like someone is out ahead of us playing a perfect game of Whac-A-Mole."

The president leaned forward, resting his forearms on his thighs. He seemed to brighten, turning his head toward Robin. "Well, we don't want to look a gift horse in the mouth. But keep me informed if you get even a sniff of anything improper."

Knowing it was her cue the briefing was over, she rose from her chair. "I'll quietly get some ears to the ground, sir."

After she left, Scalon buzzed his secretary. "Susan, set up a one-on-one meeting with Colonel Thomas for me. Tell him I have a horse I want him to look at."

The Foundation, Virginia

Both men reached up, removed earpieces. "Well, it looks like we may need to run more counterintelligence ops. The hounds will be sniffing around soon," said Dr. Abernathy.

Nick Sanders leaned back in his chair. "Perhaps we should let them find a little something in a way we can control and distance ourselves from."

***

Two Months Later, The White House

Air Force Colonel Thomas, in civilian clothes, stood looking out the window of the Oval Office, turning as he heard the president enter.

"So, what has my favorite spook unearthed?"

"Quite a bit and not so much, actually. The foundation is profoundly embedded in all scientific, technological, and social activities of the project. But they were engaged in those sorts of activities well before the arrival event. About fifteen years before, in fact."

"They've done some excellent work for every major federal department and some friendly foreign governments. Crossed all the *T*s and dotted all the *I*s." Scalon nodded.

"Aside from their involvement in the A-Squads, they've limited activities to assisting corporations and research groups. It took some digging, but I found numerous indications of previous administrations using one of their sections for some intelligence work. They've stayed to the right side of outright espionage. Just some fact-gathering and pattern analysis. I had to dig for that, because the government did the hiding, not the foundation."

Colonel Thomas drew a slim folder from his briefcase, broke the seal, and flipped a few pages before continuing. "They have a long history of making grants to individual scientists and small technology companies, some foreign but most domestic. After the arrival event, they had the reputation, connections, and people with the right skill sets to jump in with both feet."

The president paced as he listened to the report. "So, no bad apples. The barrel is sound and on our side?"

"Yes. In fact, I found some NSA recordings of them talking very positively about President Fuller's American Agenda and World Cooperation programs at several bigwig conferences. Nothing bombastic or overt, simply casual agreement when asked."

"Ah, yes. The NSA, the snake in the garden we hate but need," Scalon murmured.

* * *

Year Thirteen

"Charlie Leader to Charlie Flight. One more sweep and then match vector with Mother 27 for fuel pods by the numbers." Lieutenant Jake Bohannan loved his Sapphire Space Fighter. The only drawback was the full oxygenated liquid immersion and trilateral compression suit that allowed for 40 G acceleration without having your eyeballs smushed to a paste. After launch from an orbital hanger, flight time to the moon from Earth orbit was under half an hour with enough fuel left to put up an extended offensive fight.

His onboard AI was a finely tuned joystick with a personality. When the engineers and computer techs first inserted them in the fighters a few years back, they discovered a slight amount of separation anxiety in both the pilots and the AIs. The solution was to have pilots wear an ear- and eyepiece linkup with their AIs when away from their ships. In two more years, Jake thought, just before X-Day, he'd probably be a major, controlling a squadron of three flight wings.

Like every other fighter craft, his complement had fifteen fire-and-forget kinetic impact drones and eight laser-pumped gamma class missiles. Those babies could cook a goose through thirty inches of hardened steel after a proximity trip or before an impending enemy knockout. Through the pilots' gossip line, he'd heard some eggheads were concocting a means to harness dark energy as a weapon.

A necessary consensus had been reached. Earth focused on fast, small attack fighters versus larger and more vulnerable fixed defensive structures in space. Behemoth space-based battleships proved to be a nonstarter in every war game scenario. The only tip of the hat to fixed position offensives or defensive weaponry were the thirty-seven massive laser emplacements spread out and hidden on the moon. Mars emplacements had been considered, but there was no guarantee that the planet would be in a tactical orbital position when the time came.

AIs operated the moon-based weapons, since human operators would require supporting environmental infrastructures. Emissions leaking from a large complex might give away their locations. The moon units stayed powered down to a trickle, set to power up when unleashed by Command.

Out past the orbit of Mars, autonomous railgun weapons systems were peppered throughout the asteroid belt. Small maneuvering thrusters were used to pivot and adjust the firing angle of the rock-mounted guns. While they were single-shot systems, each one would pump out a spread of over two hundred thousand hardened steel pellets into the projected path of enemy craft. Each bullet had enough kinetic energy to punch a ten-meter impact crater on the moon or in the side of an alien ship. Even if they missed, they might cause the alien spaceships to change to vectors more favorable to Earth Space Forces.

* * *

The White House

President Scalon marveled that he was still president. A one-time exception had been approved by Congress and ratified by all fifty states three years ago to modify the Twenty-Second Amendment to the US Constitution, the one that prevented anyone from serving more than two terms as president. He'd been marginally amazed at how fast that had gone through. It seemed nobody wanted to change horses right before a battle. After X-Day, he would either serve out two more years or be dead horsemeat.

National Science Adviser William Schrift was due in at any moment with what he'd said was important news. Scalon hoped it would be good news. He was tired and needed a pickup. Schrift entered the Oval Office accompanied by the national security adviser. To the president, they both seemed a lot more relaxed than they had any right to be.

"Okay. Give me the news."

"Mr. President, one of the A-Squad teams was reviewing the contact events, starting with the first transmissions and interactions. We had dissected each one separately, but a young electronic warfare member suggested examining the transmission as a single group. I'm not sure if you remember, but the initial signal had a low power carrier wave, and the last two exhibited a handshake protocol before and after each broadcast." Schrift took a breath and explained, "Sir, we may have a way to hack their computers, or whatever they use as computers."

"And?" Scalon asked.

"Mr. President, we're going to build devices into every space fighter and put a few hundred stronger ones in Earth and Mars orbits. We're retrofitting all the AIs for control of these units. We hope to scramble their electronic brains with handshake feedback loops."

The president turned to his national security adviser. "Okay, Robin, why are you tagging along on this one?"

"Well, Mr. President, using our most advanced AI, we took another scrub on the carrier wave that accompanied the audible message. There was another text message embedded. It said, *Your choice*. We haven't a clue what that means, except perhaps we should revisit and revise the wording in Option A."

"Revisit and revise?" he repeated. "In what way?"

"Well, coupling the reference made by the aliens to the Marshall Plan, which only we received, with the newly discovered text message, I think we should make the Option A wording more of a bilateral agreement, sort of a win-win proposal, instead of a less-than-harsh conditional surrender. Change the Option A proposal so we become something more like trading partners, perhaps. We can still fall back on the original Option A if we need to. This would give us a little more cushion for dialogue before we need to decide whether to implement Strike Plan Z. The think tank team likes this approach, in light of the new message."

The president looked at Robin, searching for any sign of doubt and seeing none. "Do you think they were testing us?"

"Yes, sir, I think they were."

* * *

X-Day: Command and Control Facility

The president, advisers, and department representatives were in their second week on location, in lockdown. Other government officials and staff were scattered throughout Space Command at six redundant hardened facilities around the world. Civilian populations had been moved to pre-staged assigned locations, as had military units. The National Guard patrolled every empty city.

"Contact, sir. Three of their craft are in the Mars orbit shell."

"Let's make a deal," the president murmured. "Start the broadcast."

The same transmission beamed out from every nation in the world simultaneously with the same wording:

"We would like to know your intentions. We also want you to know we are prepared to defend our home system."

After a ten-second delay, the alien voice replied, "Have you prepared terms of surrender?"

The president paused, then asked, "Are you speaking with all world leaders?"

"No, Mr. President. All of them are listening, but we are conversing only with you as our point of contact. Not your nation, just you. Have you prepared terms of surrender?"

Control operatives in the pit were in whispered conversations with their counterparts in other countries. Single-point contact had been one of many possibilities put forward. Within a minute, the tote board filled with green up arrows. There were three red down arrows from outlier nations.

"Yes, we have prepared a document approved by all world leaders. Do you wish us to transmit it to you, or will you be arriving on the planet for a formal meeting?"

"Please transmit."

The president nodded to his communications director. "Send it."

"Transmitting, Mr. President. Sir, we expect there to be at least ten minutes before we receive a reply as they review the document."

In less than thirty seconds, however, the aliens replied, "We have received and reviewed your terms and have made some suggested changes. Please review and reply as to acceptance of the revised terms."

An AI was standing by to receive and analyze any reply from the aliens. Ten seconds later, the AI reported the only change was to strike out the provision for an exchange of ambassadors.

"Let me see a paper copy of both, please."

With SecDef and the national security adviser doing the same thing, the president reviewed the original and the amended copies side by side. Reports of other nations doing the same review were shared on the command net. After five minutes, and with the approval of all major and most minor countries, the president transmitted his response. "We see you have removed only the section on ambassador exchanges. Is that correct, no other changes?"

"That is correct, Mr. President. Your people would not survive on our planet, and we could not survive on yours, so the point is moot."

The president took a deep breath, squared his shoulders, brought his chin up, and said, "Well, it appears we have an agreement."

"Affirmative," replied the alien representative. "One last declaration remains." After a slight pause, the voice continued. "Let it be recorded, per the agreement exchanged, and as represented in fact and in purpose, we surrender to the president of the United States of America."

Silence reigned, then was broken by quiet chatter and outgoing comms. The secretary of defense looked stunned. "Did I have a stroke, or did they just surrender to us?"

Not missing a beat, the president pressed the transmit

button. "As president of the United States and on behalf of Earth, I accept your surrender."

The national science adviser slid a piece of paper to the president. *Ask them what they want to exchange* was written in large, looping cursive.

Before the president responded, the alien voice said, "As part of the agreement, we would like to offer technical information in several scientific areas, such as quantum physics, astrophysics, engineering, chemistry, and life sciences. We are prepared to download information to approved servers and data banks."

The president mentally rolled the dice and replied, "Well, that seems like a nice start. What would you like that we might provide in exchange?"

The aliens' voice replied, "We are especially interested in your arts—specifically music, humor, and fiction genres. Many of the species we trade with will find them most enjoyable. Think of us as information brokers."

President Scalon rubbed his temples. "Well, you can look inside all but the most hardened computer systems. You could take all that and more if you wanted."

"Yes," was the reply, "but that would be stealing and would ruin our reputation with other species."

"Give me a minute, please," the president said. He leaned over to his national science adviser and whispered, "Get them an Amazon account, and make it Prime. And Netflix too."

Grinning, he added, "Put it on your card, Bill."

SPACE PAINT

OR ALWAYS READ THE INSTRUCTIONS BEFOREHAND (IF YOU CAN FIND THEM)

DAVID VINER

David Viner, a founding member of the Redwell Writers group (Norwich UK), has had a number of stories published since 2007, including three in the 2021 SFN anthology. He has edited and contributed to both Redwell Writers anthologies (published in 2017 and 2020). He uses Wattpad to showcase some of his work, including Wisdom of the Ancients *(which is often at #1 in their SF category). He published two novels,* Splinters *and* Time Portals of Norwich, *in 2020, and a collection of short stories,* Time Enough for the World to End, *in 2021, and is currently working on the* Time Portals *sequel,* Time's Revenge. *Find out more at www.vivadjinn.com.*

"Oh, thank you ever so much," she said as he transferred the large wooden doll's house into her arms. "Not sure where I'm going to put it, though. I'm really running out of space."

"My goodness, Mary!" Rupert Oortman peered past her at all the, well, *stuff* that cluttered the hallway of her house. "You're not kidding."

"You should see the other rooms." She giggled. "But I

couldn't let you just throw it out. It's beautiful. Your mum's, wasn't it?"

"Yes, and her mother's before her. I just didn't have the room, and not having daughters meant it was just in the way —the boys were getting too old to be sharing a room, so we knew it was about time we did a proper clear out."

"Is there more in that?" Mary asked, seeing the large cardboard box that Rupert must have placed on the path close to the front door before ringing her doorbell.

"Yes, sorry to add to the load. It's several dolls, lots of clothes for them and so on. Must admit, I don't think that box has been touched since Mum packed everything into it years ago. That was when she moved into sheltered accommodation —didn't have any room. I can bin it, if you haven't got the space."

"Oh, no. Let me go through it first. I can throw out anything that's no good myself." She looked at Rupert's expression. "Ha! Yes, I do occasionally throw stuff out. Hard to believe sometimes, looking at all this, isn't it?"

"Um, yes. Right," he said, peering in once again, his eyebrows raised high at the boxes of dolls, toys, and other child-related paraphernalia that were packed into Mary's house. "Well, I'd better be getting off. Amy'll be giving my dinner to the dog if I don't get back soon."

"Okay, see you Monday, then."

"Yep, okay, bye." He negotiated his way past the brambles in Mary's front garden, heading back to his car.

Mary squeezed the doll's house through her hallway and into what had once been her dining room. She found a rare spot to plonk it down and gave it an all-over inspection.

"Well," she said to herself after a few minutes, "I'd say it goes back even further than Rupert's grandmother. Some of it looks distinctly Victorian, I reckon."

It had been a bit of good luck, Mary overhearing a conversation between Alison Cloverley, a work colleague several desks away in her section, and Rupert Oortman, who worked in a different department. Rupert had been asking around if anyone had wanted a large old wooden doll's house and, having discovered that Alison had two daughters, was attempting to offload it on her. But any mention of old toys, especially dolls and doll's houses, was like a magnet to Mary's ears, which had pricked up immediately. Alison had hardly needed to drag Mary into the conversation once the phrase *doll's house* had been uttered. Having worked with her for several years, Alison was fully aware of Mary's obsession with dolls and other toys.

Mary returned to the hall and picked up the cardboard box —heavier than it looked. She also saw, written on one of the top flaps, *Oortman*, followed by an address that might have been Rupert's. The postcode showed that it was certainly not far away. She took the box through to the kitchen, plonked it down on the table, and started rummaging through its upper contents. Nearly two dozen dolls—some plastic—possibly 1950s vintage—a few wooden—definitely older. "I might have trouble dating those accurately, but a damn good haul," she muttered, adding, with a shake of her head, "To think he offered to bin them!"

The box was quite deep, and there was something heavy at the bottom, underneath the pile of doll-sized furniture and clothes. She pulled it out, frowning to discover it was a can of paint.

"What is *that* doing in there?" she muttered.

The tin seemed to be older than some of the stuff that had been surrounding it, and some of its rust had tainted the clothes that had been squashed right up against it.

"Well, that can definitely go straight in the bin," she said. There were two small brown labels that had been stuck onto the otherwise bare can. Both were faded and had started to flake and peel. She held the can up to the fading evening light to read the one with the larger print and then switched the light on, as the black print on the brown label was barely legible.

"Space paint? What on earth is space paint?"

She spun the can around to read the instructions on the other label and was surprised to hear a sloshing sound within. As she did so, several pieces of label flaked off and dropped into the cardboard box.

"Not completely dried up, then," she announced to no one, and squinted at the text. Some of it was beyond deciphering, but one of the bits she could make out said *Make more SPACE in your house with SPACE PAINT! Just paint it on a wall and . . .* Whatever had come after the *and* was now lost, though another part said *. . . ly thicker to make deepe . . .*

"Ha!" she said, looking back towards the hallway. "Well, I could most definitely do with more space in this place." Even her loft space was almost completely packed.

After eating her evening meal, Mary got her phone out and tried looking up Space Paint on the internet. She found several that had the words *space paint* as part of the title. Most suggested they'd give the appearance of more space, but none actually claimed to physically increase space. So, she found a large flat-bladed screwdriver and prised the lid off the rusted can. It took a bit of effort but, once opened, it revealed a grey-green concoction which more than half-filled the tin. It didn't smell like any paint she'd ever used. There was an odour that, to her, whiffed like a cross between ozone or that of a small electric motor, such as on a train set engine after it had been sparking.

Intrigued, she hunted down a paintbrush that wasn't completely stiff with old paint. Then, finding a small piece of still unhidden wall in the hallway, at around chest height, she applied a few strokes, creating a filled circle no bigger than a small saucepan lid. For a few moments, it just sat there, making what had once been a cream wall slightly greener. Then, as it quickly dried, Mary frowned, seeing what appeared to be a depression forming in the wall at the centre of the circle. After a few more minutes, the painted hole deepened until she could put her whole fist into it.

Having a sudden panic about what it was doing, she rushed into the lounge, which shared the wall with the hallway. Like the other rooms in her house, the lounge was filled with boxes, loose toys, and doll's houses. Only one chair had enough space free to be used for its original purpose. But at that moment, Mary wasn't interested in doll's houses or toys. She ran her hand over the wall on that side, but there was no corresponding bulge.

Returning to the hallway, she found that the depression was now like a bubble—the perimeter still the saucepan lid-sized circle she had painted, but inside, it must have been the size of a very large basketball. And it hadn't stopped growing. She hunted down a torch and shone it into the hole, her mouth hanging open in wonder. If the original circle had been painted larger, she would already have been able to fit inside the bubble.

Back in the lounge, she checked the wall on that side once again. It remained as flat as it had always been.

She stopped and tried to think things through. "Am I dreaming this?" Mary asked herself. Apart from the hole in her wall, everything else felt decidedly normal—well, as normal as her house could ever be.

She decided that sleeping on it might be a good idea. So, she washed the brush and put the lid back on the paint can and, after tidying away the aftermath of her meal, sorted out the rest of what had been in Rupert's cardboard box. Very little was considered destined for the bin. Around half ten, she headed upstairs to bed—which itself had to share a room with ten other large doll's houses and their contents.

* * *

The next morning, a Saturday, arrived bright and sunny, and Mary was surprised to find the hole in the hallway wall was still present. So not a dream, then. She shone the torch into it once more and peered in. Given the small size of the entrance, she wasn't sure if it had stopped growing or not, but she estimated that it went in about three or four feet.

After breakfast, she cleared the section of the hallway below the hole and opened the paint can once more. This time, she painted a doorway-sized rectangle around the original circle and awaited the results. By lunchtime, she had added a whole new room to her house—one whose shape was, admittedly, far from resembling anything room-shaped. It was more like her own personal cave that sloped downwards from its new entrance in the hallway. At least the entrance itself had remained the rectangular shape she'd painted. Inside, illuminated by several table lamps and a string of Christmas tree lights, she could see that her handiwork had resulted in a floor that was extremely uneven, whilst the walls and ceiling were hardly any better.

Mary kept returning to the other side of the wall in the lounge to marvel that it was still completely flat. She momentarily wondered if the addition of the room had altered the structural integrity of the whole house.

"Maybe I'd better just stick to the one room," she told herself, but then squealed, "I've got my very own bigger-on-the-inside Tardis!"

Over the next few hours, a bit of experimentation showed that careful application of more paint in the corners resulted in something that was decidedly more box-shaped.

* * *

"How's the doll's house?" Rupert asked when he came past Mary's desk two days later.

"Oh, it's lovely. I haven't managed to date the really old stuff yet, though."

"Well, I'm really glad it all went to someone who appreciates it."

"Oh yes, many thanks. Some of the dolls in the cardboard box might actually be vintage."

"There was a rumour that a good many of them might have actually belonged to my great-granny Elouise, you know."

"That wouldn't surprise me. They really could be that old."

"Apparently, there was a lot more, once upon a time. Elouise claimed to have lived in a huge mansion before she'd married, but her husband had thrown out tons of her stuff after the wedding. But Gran also said that she'd once seen the house before Elouise'd got married, and it was just a normal terrace house."

"How strange," Mary said.

"Right, I'd better get on with some work, I suppose." Rupert started to walk off.

"I found the paint," Mary blurted out.

"Er, what paint?" he replied, a puzzled look on his face.

"Oh, didn't you know there was can of paint in the cardboard box?"

Rupert shook his head.

"Space paint, it was called. Something like two litres—just over half full."

"Nope, had no idea that was in there. Though the box did feel a bit heavy for just dolls and clothes," he said, adding with a grin, "Mind you, if it was that old, I expect it was well gone off!"

Mary paused and then smiled. "Yes, I expect so."

Well, she thought, there was no point in trying to explain it to Rupert—he probably wouldn't have believed her, anyway. Mary still wasn't sure she believed it herself.

* * *

It took her about three weeks of paint daubing to get her new "Tardis cave" into a more suitable shape. And that shape was just over fifty feet long and barely any less in width. The ceiling arched over her head to a height of nearly nine feet in the centre and just over six where it met the walls. Getting the floor as flat as possible had been the fun bit, but she was quite pleased with her efforts. She peered into the can of paint.

It was now pretty much empty—maybe only enough for a few more brushstrokes—so she put the lid back on and was about to chuck it in her wheelie bin when she changed her mind. Instead, Mary popped it back into that cardboard box that Rupert had delivered it in. In the bottom of the box were the scraps of label that had peeled off the can. Some of the pieces had almost turned to dust.

"Well," she said, talking to herself as usual, "I didn't really need the instructions, if there were any in all that mess. Still, it would be interesting to try to piece them together at some point and see if I can make out the name of the manufacturer. Maybe I can buy some more one day."

She closed the cardboard flaps of the box and took the box outside to her shed.

A couple of days later, she ran an extension lead from the previously buried socket in the hallway and dotted some uplighters around the room. Standing at the centre, she knew she'd more than trebled the size of her house.

Then she ordered several sets of freestanding shelving. They were delivered a few days later, and being of a practical nature, she assembled them herself. She had to spend quite a bit of time adjusting packing under the corners so that the shelves were more or less upright and didn't wobble on the still far-from-completely-flat floor. Finally, once she was sure they wouldn't fall over, she started moving her collection of doll's houses, dolls, and toys into the cave, displaying them in all their glory instead of having them crunched into boxes or piled on top of each other.

It took several weeks, but eventually the cave contained most of her collection, and the rest of her house looked, for the first time in years, like a proper house that could actually be lived in by normal people. Even the loft had been tidied up and now only contained some of the more tattered boxes and least valuable toys.

"Of course," she told herself whilst admiring her collection, "I can't really ever show this to anyone, can I?"

She wondered what they would make of an extra room that lived within a single four-inch-thick wall. By her calculations, the far end of her Tardis cave—if it had really extended that far —would have actually been located in the next-door-but-two neighbour's lounge.

She considered getting a new doorframe and door to make a proper entrance into her cave, but good though her DIY skills were, she didn't think she was quite up to fitting such a thing herself. Getting someone in to do it for her would certainly raise questions.

* * *

It was just over a year later that Mary didn't come in to work one Monday morning. She hadn't rung in to say she was ill or anything. By Wednesday, people were starting to get worried. Rupert got to hear about it when Alison, having remembered introducing them over the doll's house conversation, asked him if he'd seen her.

"No," Rupert replied. "I've only spoken to her a couple of times since then, anyway."

By Thursday morning, when the company's HR department still hadn't managed to make contact with Mary, a decision was made to inform the authorities in case some misfortune had befallen her.

On Friday morning, a police car stopped outside Mary's house and a constable got out to investigate Mary's whereabouts. After getting no answer from ringing her doorbell, which didn't appear to work, or from knocking on her front door, the policeman tried peering in the windows: front, sides, and back. However, the curtains were, in the main, closed and where he could see in, there appeared to be nothing out of the ordinary.

Returning to the front door, which was solid wood and not glazed, he lifted the flap on the letterbox and gazed inside. His eyes were met with what appeared to be a wall of splintered matchwood only inches away. Directly above the door and constructed as part of the doorframe itself was a small ornamental window. It was made up of several pieces of coloured glass that were slightly bowed outwards. One piece of glass was cracked, though it hadn't completely fallen out.

The policeman heard a door opening nearby and stood up to see the next-door neighbour, an older woman, whose face was peering over the fence at him.

"Is she okay?" the neighbour asked.

"Miss Stettheimer?" the policeman replied.

"Yes, Mary Stettheimer. Weird name. Stettheimer, that is, not Mary, of course," came the reply. "Haven't seen her for several days and was wondering if I should call you myself. But here you are anyway."

"When was the last time you saw her?"

The neighbour frowned and scratched her chin. "Well, I reckon it might have been last Thursday, or was it the Wednesday? No, could have been Friday, when she came home from work."

"But you've not seen her since then?"

"Um, no. Is she okay?"

"That's what we are trying to determine."

"Oh right," the woman said, adding, "I heard something at the weekend—Saturday evening, it was. Maybe it came from her place."

"Heard something?"

"Yes, like a *whoomp* sound, followed by hailstones. I did look around outside, but it was dark, and my Horlicks was getting cold. Totally forgot about it until now. Hmm, Stettheimer. Very weird name."

"Right, thank you."

A couple of hours later, a larger police van arrived and the front door was broken down, though they had to wrench it outwards. This was due to the hallway being packed tightly from floor to ceiling with a mass of what mostly consisted of splintered wood, though there were some lengths of bent metal and a few scraps of material mixed in with it, like small dresses made for dolls.

More officers turned up. They taped the house off and erected a tent around the front door. They also broke into the back door and found that the mass of splintered wood half-filled the kitchen as well.

Forensics spent a while picking the mass of wood apart, cataloguing what little they could identify as they went.

"Looks like dolls' clothes, sir," said Police Sergeant Lutyens to his superior. "The wood, where large enough pieces of it remain, is painted and decorated like a doll's house might be."

"Doll's house?" replied Inspector Hicks.

"Yes, we did find a couple of plastic dolls as well. Totally flattened, they were. We hear that the occupier of the premises collected them—dolls and their houses, that is—along with other toys. It was a hobby, sir. There were a few other toys found around the house."

They found Mary—or what remained of her—in the centre of the mass. It was obvious how she'd died; her body had been crushed to a pulp, though what had caused such a thing to occur was a complete mystery. Those on the case examined the rest of the house in as much detail as they could.

Once they'd cleared up the mess, they were left with what appeared to be an ordinary house in a slightly deteriorated state of repair, but the rooms themselves showed nothing out of the ordinary. The only question mark was the door-sized green-grey rectangle painted onto one of the hallway walls. It just didn't match the rest of the decor, which, although somewhat pitted from whatever had caused the mass of wood to appear, was cream in colour. The wood had been most densely packed next to the green rectangle.

Once they'd finished with the house, they turned their attention to the shed. They found very little there that was of any interest. Apart from a rusty manual lawnmower and a few other gardening tools that, going by the state of the garden, had seen little use, there was only a cardboard box. It had a name and address written on it in thick marker pen. It looked like a possible avenue for investigation, especially as the address wasn't that of the house but one a couple of miles away. Inside the box, they found an empty tin can that looked like it might have once held paint. A policeman, having prised the lid off, frowned and kept staring at the inside and then the outside of the can.

So, a few days later, Rupert Oortman found himself being interviewed by the police about the cardboard box. Without hesitation, he told them everything he knew about it. Yes, it had been him who had given it to Mary just over a year before, along with the doll's house that had originally been his grandmother's.

"Mary collected dolls and doll's houses," Rupert said.

"Yes, we know," he was told. "What about the can of paint in the box?"

"What can of paint? Oh wait, I seem to remember Mary saying that she'd found a can of paint inside the box a few days later. I never even knew it had been in there. Mum had packed the box years before, and I only checked the stuff at the top to make sure it was doll-related before giving it to Mary."

"So you never saw the paint can itself, then?"

"No, sorry. Was it important?"

"Probably not. Though it was a bit distorted. Crumpled, as if something had bashed the *inside* of the can with a hammer."

Rupert shrugged, not understanding why the officer had emphasised *inside*.

After noting everything down, Rupert was thanked for his time and allowed to go on his way.

* * *

"So, Oortman's story checks out, then?" Inspector Hicks asked a while later.

"Yes," Lutyens replied. "Though we think we've established that the green paint on the hall wall is the same as that found dried inside the tin can."

"Have they figured out what the distortions with the can are yet?"

"No, but they're not there anymore. Two days ago, the inside of the can straightened itself out. Looks completely normal now."

"Weird. Was there anything more?"

"Yes. Forensics have pieced together the remains of the label from the can."

"And?"

"Not much. It was called Space Paint. Something about making space. No idea what that means. Though we did find one other thing . . ."

"What was that?"

"A scrap of the label that mentioned it being essential to reapply a new coat at least once a year."

"Once a year?" Hicks muttered, and then tutted. "Rather rubbish paint if it needs reapplying that often. Anyway, I hardly think that's important, do you?"

Luytens shook his head. "Um, no, sir."

DRAGON HUNT
CLAUDIA BLOOD

It takes two people to steal dragon eggs.

My pura surrounded me, protecting me from the heated, acidic waters around me. The living membrane that stretched behind me as a thin cord, extending back to my ship hidden in the rocks, was my lifeline to fresh air.

Daniel, my best and only friend, floated next to me in his own pura. His ship was hidden in the same rocks mine was.

Unease and the first hint of fear gripped my stomach. Humans were not meant to be outside of their ship for long. Down here, the aquatic life was deadly. And puras could only repair so much damage.

I pushed down the fear and focused on why Daniel and I had hatched our plan to steal the eggs, sell them, and take the train to the Central Camp: it was where dreams came true. There had to be something more than the rough, deadly conditions that I'd grown up in. There were more jobs than just mining the rocky bottom for precious compounds. Central Camp was the only place where females were found. The life expectancy before I'd die and cast my clones would be much higher there. At least, I had to believe that.

All Daniel and I needed to get away was a clutch of dragon eggs.

Just ahead, the mountain which housed the dragons shimmered against the dark murkiness of the depths. Its light lured the unwary. One giant dragon was draped around the top of the mountain, staring down at the front entrance. His gills were so big I could swim inside. Even from here, his crystal heart pulsed through his translucent purple skin.

"You have the flare?" Daniel asked, not taking his gaze from the dragon.

I patted my pura's water pocket, where I had hidden two flares. "Yup." I knew he couldn't see my lips in the darkness of the ocean bottom. He'd have to wait for my answer to travel up my pura, to my ship, to his, and then down to him. Lip reading was much faster.

The plan was simple. We'd sneak in a back entrance just big enough for us to fit. There were two tunnels that led to where the dragons roosted. One came out above and at an odd angle. It would be perfect for sending the flare out the front entrance, where the dragons were sure to chase it. That was my job.

The other tunnel led to the ground level near the nests. Daniel was going to get close and then, when the dragons were distracted, he would grab as many eggs as his pura pockets would hold.

That would be enough to change both of our lives.

Getting to the back of the mountain spire was easy, but the narrow hole that led inside had jagged edges. One wrong move and we'd die.

I waited for Daniel to look at me. "Are you sure about this?"

He nodded. His lips tightened. "My pura is rejecting me already. If I can't make it to the Central Camp, I'll be dead before I'm sixteen."

To be honest, either one of us could die at any time. Mining was dangerous. The clone gangs in town were even more so. The fact that Daniel and I had no other clones to even the odds made us targets. Two could not stand up to ten or a dozen or more.

Taking this risk was the only way to have a chance. I nodded. "Send a message when you're in place."

"No matter what happens, this is worth the risk." Daniel ducked into the opening. His words, "I'm glad you are my friend," echoed to me a few moments later.

I took a deep breath, shook off the feeling of foreboding that had lodged in my chest, and focused on surviving this adventure.

I needed to do something to make sure my pura cord would travel smoothly down the tunnel without snagging on the rocks. As I got farther from the ship, the bubble around me would get smaller and extend the cord behind me. I didn't want the sharp rocks cutting my cord. If I couldn't grab it and reconnect it in a timely manner, I'd suffocate.

I placed the cord carefully as I went, finding the spots between the rocks or making room where I could.

Finally, I made it to the space above, where I could see the dragons flitting around the next chamber. I peered over its edge.

Below, the fist-sized eggs glittered in the slant of sunshine which had somehow found its way into the cave. Daniel hunched behind a rock near the nest.

I extended the flare and planted the stick so its flash would fly toward the main entrance. There was one last thing I needed to do. I shifted my pura color to match the rocks here. Matching the rock should help hide me from the dragons if they came up here. I was the only one I knew who could change the color of my pura. I'd never told anyone. Being different would've put a target on my back.

"Ready?" I asked softly.

I watched Daniel carefully. Even with the delay, the message should be to him. He didn't seem to hear me. The first wave of panic kicked me in the gut. Had I not been loud enough, or had one of us lost our connection to our ship? I shivered at the thought. If our line of communication was closed, I still needed to send out the flare and time it when he was ready.

Daniel hadn't moved since I'd been watching him. *He must be ready.*

I flipped the flare on and pulled back so it was fully in the water. The fuse crackled and popped and burned. The squeaks, grunts, and chatter of the dragons in the cave stopped suddenly as the flare sparked to life. It brightened and then propelled itself out of the cave.

I concentrated on being invisible and not moving. This was the most dangerous part. A small rip in my pura could be dealt with, but too big a tear was a death sentence. I stayed frozen, thinking rock thoughts as the cave erupted into a shrill multinote cry and the dragons streaked out of the cave to give chase.

One small female wrapped her tail around me. She stared at the six dragons wrestling near the entrance. I could see the delicate play of her gills frantically pulling in fluid and the ruby glow of her crystal heart pumping blood through her system.

She looked at the rock she perched upon: me. Her head tilted as it inched closer to mine. Could she tell I wasn't a rock? She swayed back and forth, turning her head one way, then the other, getting closer and closer. Her mouth opened and her tongue flicked.

The loud squeal of two dragons grappling each other, each trying to get out of the cave first, distracted her. She shifted uneasily to watch them. But she kept flicking her eyes between them and me. When the opening was clear, she launched herself with a shriek, leaving behind several small punctures in my pura which instantly repaired themselves.

The cave was clear of any able-bodied dragons. I could see

their backs outside as they guarded the cave's main entrance, hissing and chattering. The rest must have scrambled to catch our flare as it zoomed through the fluid.

With great care, I backed out of the room and slid through the twisted cave to the split. This was where Daniel would meet me. Worry tugged at me. Daniel still hadn't responded. Had he feared being heard, or was something amiss? I examined his cord, and my heart sank.

It looked oddly flat. I followed the cord, hoping it was just a weird angle. I turned the next corner and the pura ended. Ended! Puras don't end. But it had, as if it had been sheared off. Fear soured my stomach.

I grabbed the end of his pura. It would soon start retracting back to his ship. Without the connection to a human, the ship would self-destruct, sending out Daniel's clone eggs.

I kept going to where I'd seen him last. He hunched over the nest, oblivious to the fact he was cut off from the ship. His cord slowly contracted back to him. I couldn't yell, or the dragons would attack both of us. I could only make my way to him and hope it would be in time.

He absorbed another egg.

A shriek drew my gaze. That dratted female flew straight at Daniel. She circled, shrieking and diving at him. She scored a hit, leaving long scratches on his pura. The other dragons' shrieks changed and glittering eyes turned back in our direction.

"Daniel!" I called, but realized he could not hear me since he was separated from his ship. I suctioned a rock and threw it at the little female, hitting her in the midsection. She and the rock flew back.

Daniel jumped at the crash and turned to look at me.

I waved frantically, trying to get him to come back, holding up the end of his pura that still connected to the ship. But he turned his back, reaching for yet another egg.

Damn him, they'd be no good to us if he was dead.

Daniel's pura cord pulled from my hands. Time was running out for him.

I sent another rock careening into the cave at the dragon showing interest in Daniel by the nest. The extra flare! I set it up and aimed at the front entrance.

The cave was filling with the smaller, faster dragons who came chittering and swooping at Daniel. I kept a steady barrage of rocks going. Even small rocks seemed to provoke them as they snapped at each other in annoyance. The first large dragon hit the entrance as the flare came to life and barreled toward the doorway.

Luck was with us, and the flare hit the big dragon full in the chest, sending him careening out of the cave. He crashed against the rocks outside and shattered. A cry went up as the dragons went to collect pieces of him, forgetting us for the moment.

I made it to Daniel's side and tugged at him. He shrugged me off weakly, and then I saw that a rock had fallen and shattered his leg. The bottom of his pod was filled with his blood and his eyes were glazed. His cache was full of dragon eggs. A treasure trove. Enough to get us to Central Camp.

There was still a chance. If I could merge our pods, I could treat his wounds and supply him with oxygen. I touched his pod and tried.

But it didn't work. Maybe his sickness made the connection impossible. All that was left to try was to suction onto his pura and pull him back through the passageway.

A small bubble message budded off his pod and adhered to mine. My throat closed. This couldn't be the end for Daniel. I'd only be able to read his message back at the ship.

He slumped in his pura. I wished I could see his face, and that I could press on the wound and stop the bleeding; that somehow I could save my best friend. But the bubbles between us wouldn't allow me to touch him.

I made it to our ships and tried to connect Daniel to his. But as his pod touched his ship, it disintegrated. His body hissed in the acid water. He was dead.

I'm not sure how long I sat on the ground, staring without seeing Daniel, but when I came to myself, Daniel's remains had been reclaimed by the water. I had to grab the dragon eggs, or his death would have been for nothing.

One by one, I added the eggs to my ship's cache. When I was done, I waited. Daniel's ship would cast his clones. I was going to grab them, even though it was frowned upon. I didn't want the dragons to feast upon them.

The ship's pod cracked. A low hiss meant the water was eating the inside. When the shell erupted, I grabbed the thousands of tiny pods floating in the water. Those tiny pods had clone eggs and a tiny ship seed. If a pod survived long enough, the human, tree, and ship would all grow into adults.

If I lived that long, maybe I would see Daniel again in the form of one of these clones.

I merged. My pura merged with the ship's hull, leaving me free to walk to the central tree that supported it.

I pulled out Daniel's final message. It had been encoded by Daniel's ship. My ship could read it. A wash of pain and anger rushed through me.

I tucked the note into the ship and his words echoed through the ship.

"It only takes one to go to Central Camp. Don't give up the dream. Go without me."

UNSPEAKABLE WORDS
PHILIP CAHILL

London, 2225

The record of the London android riots of 2205, a remarkable audiovisual document, had been created from video surveillance and police body cam images. The body cam images were particularly disturbing. One sequence showed a group of officers approaching a dozen or so rioters who were smashing shop windows on Oxford Street. The group leader ran ahead of his colleagues, trying to calm the situation down. One of the androids attacked.

The policeman was punched to the ground and then subjected to a barrage of vicious kicks to the body and the head. The officer died within seconds of the start of the attack and, even when it was obvious that the man was dead, the android continued his onslaught. A heavy calibre shell from a police assault rifle stopped the attacker. The shell blew away most of his head.

The twentieth anniversary of the riots meant that it was now being widely streamed. Karen watched it on the plane as she headed towards London. It made her nervous. Tensions between the android and human communities had eased since the riots, but there was still sporadic violence in parts of London.

* * *

Karen strode into the hotel and approached the desk. The only way she could tell that the receptionist at the Carlton House Hotel was not human was that he couldn't make eye contact with her. The detailing was perfect, but he was clearly an android. His eyes were constantly moving as he processed the telepathic flux that passed through his brain. She knew her anxiety was irrational; this was a luxury hotel, after all, and only a small percentage of androids had been involved in the riots. She decided to make an effort to put these thoughts out of her mind. She was here to do a job.

"I'm Mrs. Collaroy," she said. "I have a reservation for the weekend."

He verified her identity with a facial scan and ordered two humanoid automatons to facilitate the reception process. One went to her taxi to retrieve her luggage, and the other asked her to follow him through the richly carpeted atrium towards the main staircase.

By the time they had reached the Calypso suite on the first floor, her luggage had been delivered. She told the machine that she didn't need him to help her unpack. He wished her a pleasant stay and left the room.

The suite had a river view. She opened the french windows of the salon and moved out onto the balcony, walking past the exterior dining table towards the stone balustrade and looking out at the Thames. She glanced at her watch. There was about an hour to wait before her meeting with Wilfred Friedman. Normally, she would never agree to a business meeting in a hotel suite, but she had known Friedman ever since finishing her postgraduate studies in Lexical Semantics at Berkeley.

* * *

Friedman, an antiquarian book dealer of about seventy-five, was a vain man. He disliked revealing his true age. He still had a full head of hair, which he had expensively styled and subtly dyed, and he also dressed well. In a flattering light, he could pass for someone much younger. He arrived at the Calypso suite with a young assistant, Jeremy. She hadn't met Jeremy before, but she wasn't surprised. Friedman's assistants, who were always chosen for their looks, tended to last only about eighteen months. Jeremy carried a large attaché case, which he placed on a lectern that had been set up in the salon. He then left the suite, watched closely by the old man.

"Beautiful, isn't he?" said Friedman.

"He's younger than my son, Wilfred. Now c'mon, you haven't flown me across the Atlantic and set me up in this fabulous suite just to show me your boyfriend."

"He's not my boyfriend."

"Okay, let's get down to business. Do you want to show me the book?"

Friedman pulled two pairs of white cotton gloves from his pocket. He pulled on one set and handed the other to Karen. He opened the case and carefully removed a leather-bound book. It was about the size of a large dictionary. He opened the volume at a page near the centre.

"What am I looking at?" asked Karen.

"One of the few pages with text we can actually read. The book dates from 2075, and I acquired it last year together with twenty-five other books from the estate of Naudot, the tech billionaire. It's being auctioned early next week, so you've got the weekend to decipher it."

"What? You told me this was just a preliminary examination. There's no way I could decode a whole book in a weekend."

"I think you can," said Friedman. "You're probably the

only one who can. Once you've found the key, a computer can handle the rest. It's a bit of a long shot, I know, but I've had a lot of interest in this piece, and a decoding key and some academic gobbledygook from someone with your reputation could add a significant chunk of money to the asking price. I've organised the same range of computing facilities that you have at Berkeley and a security cordon around the suite for the whole time you're going to be here."

"How many experts have looked at this?" she asked.

"A few of my in-house people and a guy I know at Cambridge, but basically, you're the only one I trust to take a close look at it."

"Can you give me some context? Do you know anything about the book? About the previous owners?"

"I'd rather not say anything at the moment. You're cracking a code here. Just think of it as a piece of mathematics," said Friedman.

* * *

When Friedman had gone, Karen set up a video screen on the back wall of the salon, scanned the title page of the book, and contacted her AI.

"Emily, I've just sent you some information about a book I want to examine. Could you track down a digital copy and a summary of the research literature, and forward them to me?"

"Searching . . . There is no digital version available. In addition, there does not appear to be any literature on previous studies of the work."

"What about previous owners?" asked Karen.

"Apart from Wilfred Friedman, one previous owner listed."

"What, in a hundred and fifty years? Give me the previous owner's name."

"A Mr. Naudot, who acquired it twenty years ago," said Emily.

Karen scanned the book with her phone and began to dictate as she examined the physical copy on the lectern.

"Leather-bound volume, 25×6×16 centimetres, containing 1750 pages and probably weighing about 1.6 kilograms. The binding is unmarked and is in excellent condition, given the age of the article. The pages are exclusively text, according to the scan. Just leafing carefully through a few pages . . . That seems to be the case.

"The pages are blocks of text arranged in paragraphs and paginated with arabic numerals on the bottom right-hand corner of each page. Apart from page 795, the text appears in a script I don't recognise, but the form of the text looks similar to a truncated Latin script. There are conventional-looking punctuation marks and other marks I don't recognise, but judging by their position relative to the characters, these seem to be additional punctuation indicators. There are no variations in character size. The sentences are also very long."

She initiated an analysis of the characters. She established that a twenty-six-character set had been used, and the patterns revealed by the analysis showed patterns similar to natural languages. Therefore, the book was not composed of a series of random symbols.

She decided to start with the text on page 795. It contained two long sentences of apparent gibberish written in twenty-first century British English.

* * *

She tapped her phone and asked Emily to get Friedman for her. It seemed to take the AI a long time.

"Wilfred, can you tell me why there is no record of this thing anywhere, no details of who owned it before Naudot, no academic studies, nothing, not even a press report?"

"Karen, I'm a little busy at the moment."

"Okay. When you're less busy, can you call me back?"

Friedman made a noncommittal grunt and ended the call. Karen looked at the sentences in English again and examined the surrounding sentences, skimming over the characters. She photographed the page and sent the image to Emily.

"Emily, please analyse the morphology of the textual characters on this page. Pay particular attention to the sentences immediately preceding and immediately succeeding the text in English."

"Working . . . Here is a revised image of the text. I have also extrapolated from your earlier scans and the age of the artefact. I think that there is a good likelihood that there is a concealed portal in the spine of the book."

"Fine, try to verify and, if possible, connect to it," said Karen. She examined the new image. There were now fewer words on the page, but all the characters were in English. Karen dictated some additional notes as she continued to leaf through the pages.

"The text has been encoded using a character set to make them unreadable. In effect, the shapes of the letters in the original English character set have been modified. I have now managed to recover some decoded text. Now trying to see if it is possible to connect to a portal in the book."

Emily signalled that a portal was available, and she was connecting to it. Karen closed the book and ran her fingers along the grain of the leather cover.

"Alert," said Emily. "Leave the immediate vicinity of the object."

Karen didn't respond verbally, she just moved away from the lectern towards the door. By the time she had gone through it, the hotel's fire alarm went off. She kept moving along the corridor, her eyes searching for the emergency exit.

"I have neutralised the threat," said Emily. "You may now return to your suite. I am explaining the threat to the hotel. There is someone on the way to see you."

Karen leant against the wall of the corridor as she thought things through. She called Friedman.

"Why was this thing booby-trapped? If it wasn't for the security protocol built into my AI, I could've been—I don't know—I could've been killed!"

Wilfred asked, "Calm down. Can you explain?" She saw the lift door open and someone running towards her.

"Gotta go, Wilfred. Talk to you later," said Karen.

"Mrs. Collaroy, I'm the safety officer. Are you okay?"

"Yes. There seems to have been a problem with something in my room. My AI advises that the problem has now been resolved and I can go back to my suite."

"Could I ask that you let me have a link to your AI? I must insist that you stay here. I'm sure you understand. I must be certain that there is no danger to you or the other guests."

"Sure."

The fire alarm stopped while she waited. She sat on the corridor's thick carpet. Her phone signalled a call from Friedman.

* * *

Karen stood behind Friedman as he leafed through the book. All the pages were blank.

"What have you done?" he asked.

"I told you. The alarms went off and I got the hell out of here. The manager guy has told me I've gotta leave. So, y'know. I'm going to Heathrow and jumping on the first jet taking me home."

"I'll deal with him," said Friedman. "You get that text back."

"Nope. Going home, Wilfred."

"I haven't been entirely honest with you. I need your help with this."

"Start, Wilfred. Start right now being honest. Did you know this thing could explode?"

"*Explode* is rather an emotive term. Let's just say *rapidly deconstruct.*"

"I'd rather not have my ass rapidly deconstructed."

"You were in no real danger."

She was about to swear at him when she noticed that Emily had sent her a status report about the book. It was clear that the object was no longer dangerous.

"Wilfred, that honesty you promised me? Still waiting."

"The book belonged to a member of an android religious sect. Well, actually, the founder of the sect."

"Who?"

"He had many names. The earliest one he was known by was Ariel. He was a non-corporeal android. He lived in storage media until he learned how to create a containment field that would allow him to move around. He was also a particularly nasty individual, a toxic mixture of arrogance, paranoia, and a pathological hatred of non-android life."

"I thought androids were atheists," said Karen. "Something to do with their belief that if a consciousness can exist in an artificial neural substrate, then there is no God the Creator, and no immortal soul."

"The sect believed in a non-reductionist view of consciousness. That the body and the soul were two distinct elements."

"Okay. That sounds pretty conventional."

"That bit, yes. But the sect also believed that biological entities are an aberration. The essential purity required to be worthy of God's love is only possible in post-biological beings. These are not people that any sane person would want to meet."

"The book is?" asked Karen.

"A clandestine religious text that, I think, preaches about the obscenity of pre-android life forms and calls for the purification of the universe."

"Which is why the text was encoded. Hang on a minute. Why text in the first place? Why not an encrypted digital file?"

"Text is simpler to create and hide. The sect also had a belief in the notion of a book as a sacred object. Something that physically represented the word of God."

Karen's eyes widened. She couldn't keep the sarcasm out of her voice.

"So, God is in this too? This time, an android god that thinks we're obscenities that must be purged." She spoke into her phone. "Emily, can you find some information on how I might recover the text?"

"I'll just go and wave some money about in the hotel manager's office," said Friedman. "Back in about ten."

* * *

It was the challenge of recovering the text that kept her working on the book. She looked at the image Emily had constructed. At least Karen had a page of unencoded words. The words she had to work with were very complex. The writer had used a high-level register of complicated multicomponent words wrapped in a framework of complex grammar.

"Karen," said Emily, "I have a solution to the text problem. The words have not been erased. It's just that the colour of the font has been changed to match the colour of the page."

"How does that help?"

"The pages have been extensively exposed to light over the past hundred and fifty years because the book has been read many times. We have established that the book has some kind of symbolic significance. It's a bit like a bible that is read from during religious ceremonies. There is enough difference in shade between the characters and the pages for me to reconstruct the original text."

"You're saying the original form of the book can be reconstructed?"

"Theoretically, but I don't have enough information about the structure of the object to be able to give you a definitive answer."

* * *

"Wilfred," said Karen, "I've decoded the characters of the text, but I've got more work to do before you can read it, because the language is so complex. In effect, the real meaning of the manuscript is still hidden from prying eyes."

"This is good. The more mysterious this thing remains, the more it's worth. Besides, no one will really want to read the crap this sect has written. I just want you to put the text back on the pages."

Karen stared into Wilfred's eyes. She fought to keep the irritation out of her voice.

"I don't know yet if that will be possible. I need to get someone to examine the structure of the object. I have got a digital copy in readable form, so facsimiles could be printed."

"This object is unique, and you've ruined it," said Friedman.

"Think, Wilfred. Use your money brain. You're not remotely concerned about the intrinsic value of this artefact, are you? You don't give a rat's ass, right?"

"Yes, I do. You've ruined it for me, money-wise."

"C'mon. You've got the original, and now you've got a copy. Your customer base has just hugely increased. Listen, you'll be able to sell the original to a museum or a university, and if you print five hundred or so copies and wrap them in some fancy leather, you'll still make a huge amount from this."

"Yes, but not as much as by selling the original at auction. I want this thing restored. You said you know someone who could examine the structure of the object."

"No, I didn't. I said I *need* to get someone to examine it. Wait, we're missing something here."

"What?" asked Friedman.

"This thing was written by an android, right?"

"So?"

"Is he still alive? This Ariel guy?"

"He was the leader of the sect. We don't know if he was the author. Besides, you really don't want to approach someone like that."

"I'm not going anywhere near him, but that doesn't mean he can't be contacted. You could use an intermediary. Someone without a bloodstream. Someone less obscene than you and me."

"There's a slight problem with that idea," said Friedman.

"Yeah?"

"Anyone who knew what this text is really about would find it offensive that a human was trying to examine the sacred text."

"Fine. Let me see what I can do on my own."

* * *

They were sitting in the main bar of the hotel. Wilfred was sipping a large scotch and scanning the bar, looking at the other guests. He was an inveterate people-watcher. Karen left her drink untouched on the table. She watched the pleasure boats on the river as they cruised past the hotel.

"My AI has managed to restore the original text," Karen explained, "so the book is exactly how it was when you first showed it to me."

"Wonderful. I knew you'd be able to do it," said Wilfred. "I'm going to try and bring the auction forward." He all but rubbed his hands together over this. "There's so much interest in this thing. I really don't want to wait."

"I've also looked at the decoded text again."

"You want to come along to the auction?" asked Wilfred.

"No. You said it'll be streamed. I want to get home, now

the job's done. I can see it on the plane. Are you interested in what the text actually says?"

"Not really. I just want to sell the bloody thing."

"I've written up my report, given you the English text and my summary of what I think it's about."

"Some sort of black mass gibberish, I suppose."

"It's much worse than that," said Karen. "There's a section at the end of the book. It seems to be an incantation to a deity they call the God of the Dust World. A barren wasteland devoid of biological life. I didn't get it all, but it's a call to rise up and purge the Earth of impurities."

"What, killing us all off?"

"Yes, the entire human race. And there's something else about the incantation."

"Do I want to hear this?" asked Wilfred.

"The incantation has a telepathic component."

"So?"

"The alarm that went off when Emily connected to the book. I went through the analysis that she produced. The thing was only about to explode because my impure hand was touching it when the connection to the portal was made. The real purpose of connecting to the portal was to send out a wide-area telepathic broadcast."

"To do what?" asked Wilfred.

"To represent God speaking to his disciples in telepath. The problem is that if I've caused a broadcast, there may be some metadata attached to it that could identify me. Will this make me a target for some religious nutcase? Am I in danger, Wilfred?"

"Don't know," said Wilfred. "Let me see how I can spin this. Nothing too alarming, just a little *je ne sais quoi* to help me up the reserve price."

She saw he had no interest in her safety at all. Karen wanted the throw the contents of her glass into Friedman's face. Instead, she rose from her chair and left the bar.

THANK YOU

We hope you enjoyed this collection. The Science Fiction Novelists invite your feedback. If you are interested, please join us on our Facebook group page.

www.facebook.com/groups/science.fiction.novelists

Printed in Great Britain
by Amazon

42856769R00116